NOT TOO NARROW
. . . NOT TOO DEEP

NOT TOO NARROW
. . . NOT TOO DEEP

RICHARD SALE

PILGRIMS BOOK SERVICES
TASBURGH NORWICH ENGLAND

Originally published in the United Kingdom
by Cassell & Co. Ltd. 1936
Three impressions

Paperback edition by Corgi Books, a division
of Transworld Publishers, 1965

This hardback edition 1984

ISBN: 0 946259 12 7

Photoset by Waveney Typesetters, Norwich
and printed by The Thetford Press Ltd., Thetford, Norfolk.

FOREWORD

This astonishing little book first appeared in the late 1930s, and then again in the 1960s, and many of us read it. Then it went out of print, but a friend of mine had kept a battered copy which I used to borrow every few years to re-read. Here is the myth for our time. Here is the Great Theme – the emergence out of the nowhere (or the everywhere) of one who carries absolute strength, love, certainty and command, and can therefore enter into the darkest situations, among the most depraved types of human beings and bring an impulse for transformation and redemption. There is in every soul the eternal, imperishable kernel of spirit, the seed-point which can fructify and open and flower. This concept we may grasp intellectually. To make it vivid and real is the work of fiction, art and drama. This book, this archetypal tale, does just that for us, and sparks off in the soul of the reader the same operation for transformation of self into Self.

Here we have an example of the Myth – and all myths are variants of the one great tale of man's descent into the darkness of separation and his redemption through the power of love awakening the secret centre of divinity within the heart.

When Keith Ellis first told me of his venture in founding the Pilgrims Book Services, in order to republish lost treasures concerned with the new/old vision of the spiritual nature of man and the universe, he asked me for suggestions of old titles that might appropriately be revived for our time. At once I remembered Richard Sale's *Not Too Narrow . . . Not Too Deep*, and again I borrowed the battered paper-back and sent it to him. It rejoices my heart that he has re-published it. May it carry to many the real inspiration that great art and great tale-telling can bring. It is about healing in the truest sense, the making whole of our fallen humanity.

Sir George Trevelyan

FOR ARLINE

THE ESCAPE PARTY

HENRY MOLL	An English jewel thief, and leader of the escape
RICHARD PENNINGTON	An American professor convicted of peacetime espionage
LOUIS BENET	A Frenchman convicted of rape
CARL WEINER	A German convicted of sedition
RUDOLPH FLAUBERT	A French murderer and pathological case
JESUS TELEZ	A Spanish smuggler
JACQUES DuFOND	A young French petty thief
JAMES DUNNING	An English bigamist
GEORGE VERNE	A French murderer
PHILIP LaSALLE	An American medico, convicted of manslaughter. The narrator, and

JEAN CAMBREAU

Part I

*Flight is a matter of money, but
freedom is the will of God*

Nine out of ten of those coast fishermen who put in at St
Pierre and offer escape are rascals. I remember the horror
I felt when I first learned that they trafficked in other
men's misery. They'd offer their boat for your escape.
When you got on it and put out to sea they'd stab you in
the back; and when you were dead they'd disembowel
you, cut out the metal capsule with your precious money,
and throw your body overboard where the sharks and
barracuda made short work of it. You have to hide your
money in your body, you see, because that is the only safe
place you have.

But Gruno was reliable. He didn't make a business of
escape. He would only tie up at the dock when his catch
had been meagre and he needed money badly.

It was dangerous for him to do it. He worked it pretty
safely though. He used himself only as agent. He had no
part in the actual escape. This was the technique: Gruno
would name a sum. For that sum he would promise to
have a boat and supplies secreted at some given spot on
the north coast. Then he was finished. It was up to you to
reach the spot, find the boat, and embark.

It was Henry Moll who first contacted Gruno. Moll had
been in the colony for five years, and had survived its
rigours amazingly well. He was a cold, self-sufficient man.
The only time I ever heard him laugh was when he told
me about the time he had tried to rob the Bank of
England. I laughed too because it was a very funny story.
Otherwise Moll had been a flawless machine. He didn't
live. He operated. . . . He'd been a jewel thief on the
continent. He'd flown in the war. Very well, too; his

1

record was nine enemy planes. He never talked about that much. He'd been – he told us – a poor thief because they had caught him. At Marseilles.

I don't think Moll was afraid of anything. He towered over me, must have been inches over six feet tall. He had the chiselled nose of an æsthete, the thin mouth of a sadist, and the empty eyes of a corpse. You could never see the thought behind his eyes. When you looked at his face, you saw nothing but raw cynicism. He scoffed at religion, was an ardent atheist. Yet he was eccentric enough always to carry with him a battered Bible, for the sheer delight he derived in mocking it. He never showed emotion. When you addressed him his lips curled sneeringly, and his whole manner became instinctively offensive.

Moll, on learning of Gruno's proposition, came to me and told me of it. He added: 'I have five hundred francs to squander on an escape, and I intend to take advantage of the offer. Since Gruno's price is five thousand francs it means that I will have to surround myself with nine other fools who possess five hundred francs each and are mad enough to spend it this way. I am asking you to join me because you are intelligent and a weakling. It will be understood from the start that I am to run the entire show. . . .' A curl of the lips then. 'If you own five hundred francs and are interested, consider yourself a member of the party. Otherwise you can rot in hell with my best wishes.'

I had the five hundred francs. I joined the party.

The next member was Jacques DuFond.

You cannot think of DuFond and Moll together. Moll was fierce, adamant, he seemed deathless. DuFond was young and immature; he cringed when you spoke to him. He regarded existence with furtive, frightened eyes. He always sought protection in a stronger champion. He was a *môme*, but not from desire. Homosexuality had been the easiest way for him. He would not have lived

2

otherwise – he did not have the makings of a man. Petty larceny had brought him to the colony; the astonishing thing was that he'd had the nerve to commit the felony in the first place. He was slight, but well-proportioned; pink-skinned, light wavy hair, soft hands. A nice-looking boy, perhaps a trifle effeminate. His expression was that of a field mouse. . . . I had found a field mouse once behind a barn door, sitting quietly on some planking. For a brief moment we had come face to face, that mouse and I. We were both curious, both a trifle startled. The mouse had large soft eyes, watery as though from exopthalmic goitre. I was a giant; the mouse a midget. Ergo, when reason had told him this, the mouse fled in terror. . . . That was like DuFond. You could see him think it all out, watch the thoughts that flitted by in his eyes, see the fear, suspicion, distrust, hate. He was too young for the colony. Had he not come out he would have passed his way quietly and never engaged in dangerous matters. Moll took the boy on because he was a weakling. Moll, of course, had definite plans for the escape, and he wanted no interference from somebody with a spine. . . . If I had one, it was long dormant. I was old enough to avoid responsibility; but it was my physical weakness that Moll had referred to. He liked to taunt me about my hernia. 'LaSalle, you're an egg-shell, an old empty egg-shell, and one day you'll rot so far your shell will split and your stomach will drop down into your feet, and then you'll writhe in agony while you die. I should like to see it.'

How ironic in the end. DuFond the midget was destined to live, while Moll's great white bones sank deep into the mud on the floor of the Atlantic.

The fourth to join us was Richard Pennington. I knew him only slightly when Moll first approached him. Yes, he had five hundred francs. Yes, he would like to escape. 'You see,' he said, 'I've been working on a comprehensive survey of the French penal system, and I want very much to return to the United States so that I can finish it and

3

publish it.' . . . He was an American, fifty-five years old. It was nothing short of miraculous that he was still alive. He was in the last stages of pulmonary tuberculosis; his lungs must have been shredded. He had been in the colony ten years, convicted of peacetime espionage in 1924 while travelling abroad on vacation from teaching in America. There was no doubt at all about his guilt, but his motive was absurd. He'd been approached by military agents and asked to co-operate. He was so flattered he had accepted. They caught him easily. . . . Pennington had the face of a practical scientist and the eyes of a dreamer. He told me that he had once taught Sociology at the University of Virginia. It seemed grotesque at the time; but there was something essentially superior in him even then. I think his penal survey might have been brilliant.

Louis Benet was the fifth to join. He had been committed to the colony for raping an eight-year-old child. After he was caught the police traced other monstrosities to him. The queer part was that he was a married man – had two young daughters of his own. His wife had divorced him after his conviction.

He was not mad. Quite sane, on the contrary. He knew what he had done, knew it was horrible. It made no difference. He had no desire to change.

Benet had a dark oily skin, olivey in hue, and his head was bald through the centre with two tufts of grey on each side of the hairless streak. He had a habit of dry-washing his hands when he spoke to you; he always bowed and scraped obsequiously. Yet all the while you knew what a beast he had been and what a beast he could be again. He was sleek, almost fat. With natural talents for avarice, his capsule was well filled. (Convicts, you see, make money in prison. There is the regular pay, and then the extras, tips for running keepers' errands, gambling winnings, and all you can steal.) . . . 'Savings for my start in the world,' he would say humbly, 'my new start. When I leave I am

4

going to begin all over again. I am going to have a new life.'

The sixth and seventh members of the expedition were Jesus Telez and Rudolph Flaubert.

Telez, a sullen uncommunicative Spaniard, was twenty-five years old. Moll told me that he had been caught smuggling foodstuffs across the Andorra border. He was very religious, a Catholic. He wore a crucifix around his neck. He had faith in his God, but not in his fellow men; he was not aware of the incongruity.

Flaubert was pathetic. The others hated him because they feared him. Perhaps – being a medico – I understood him. They saw him as a lunatic; I realized he was a pathological case. He was thirty-seven years old, and a *libéré*; that is to say, he had served his prison term and was now living out his term of exile in the colony. He was the only *libéré* in the party.

He had suffered (and was still suffering) a severe nervous breakdown, the most pernicious disease a man can have. It had given him a vicious persecution complex, which had finally caused him to strangle his wife; he believed she was ridiculing him with her unfaithfulness. His mental condition had affected all of him. His body was as gnarled as his mind, and he had no hair on his head at all. There was only a glistening expanse of skin across the skull, ubiquitously rosy from the sun. His face looked like an egg perched on a body of swamp-root.

Carl Weiner was the eighth man, a German. He had been convicted of sedition six years before. He cultivated an irascible exterior, feeling that it lent him formidability. Men avoided him. He dramatized any episode which made him appear a leader. You should have seen him when the Saar re-united with the Fatherland! It was a major triumph for him. He was a bore.

The ninth man was named James Dunning. He is of no importance in the story because he did not live to take part in it. He never reached the coast.

5

So far we were a wretched crew. And Moll loved it! I could see it all turning in his mind. He needed five thousand francs to get Gruno's boat and supplies; all right, all right. Get men who were weak and sick and rotting. There was the chance that they would fail to reach the boat. There was the chance that they would die in the boat after they reached it – the boat would be small; the more who died, the less dissension. The more dead, the greater chance for the living.

We were shy a man. The tenth. The last five hundred francs. . . . There were plenty of men to choose from, but Moll was very wary.

George Verne wanted to come. He had learned of the escape through DuFond. Moll refused to let him. I had watched the scene between them. They had faced each other like animals – teeth bared, fists clenched. That was the trouble. Neither feared the other. And Moll could not risk a man who was not afraid of him. Verne would have been a menace to his authority.

It was Verne who had taken DuFond under his shelter, protected him. In return DuFond had been *môme* for Verne. In the colony such relationships are not uncommon. Neither DuFond nor Verne was a homosexual naturally. But Verne was something of a satyr. He had to have his relief; there were no women there. As for DuFond, he was young and weak and the association had its benefits. Verne took care of him, fought his fights, gave him money. It was the easiest way so the boy took it. No perverts, you see, either of them. One wanted relief; the other security and a champion.

As in many of these cases, the relationship affected Verne deeply. He felt real affection for DuFond after a while – probably the only affection he had ever shown anybody. Where DuFond was concerned, he became a weakling. Otherwise, he was brutally strong. Had there been a woman accessible, of course, he would have thrust DuFond aside: as he did so, later.

When the word got around that Moll had refused Verne the rest of us agreed it was a good thing. He would have made trouble; no doubt of that. As to his turning informer, there wasn't a chance of that. Informers don't live long in a penal colony. They meet death in apparently 'accidental' ways – but quickly. Then, too, there is always the hope, up to the last, of sharing in an escape. No, Verne wouldn't tell.

But the tenth man. Who was it to be?

2

Then Jean Cambreau appeared. Who he was, where he came from, not one of us knew. It was possible, among all the convicts, that some of us should not have known him. But it was almost inconceivable that he should have been a total stranger to all nine of us.

He appeared unexpectedly, placed his five hundred francs in Moll's big hand, and said: 'Take me with you, please.'

No pleading, no begging, no whining; no fervent listing of his merits and how much he could do to make the escape successful. Nothing but: 'Take me with you,' spoken in tones of firm confidence which was unnatural to a convict.

And Moll – who had leered at hopefuls, burned their ears with insults and wished them decay in the cesspools where they belonged – Moll said simply: 'All right.'

It seemed contrary to his make-up to assent so readily, without some cynical observation, without a query as to who the man might be, how he had learned of the proposed flight, where he had come from, what his crime had been, where he was going. . . .

I could not understand it. Cambreau had done nothing but ask to go.

Well, we needed a tenth man. . . . Now we had him. We were to set off for the coast, by ones and twos, next morning.

3

It was twilight when we reached the beach, Cambreau and
I. We could see it while we were still deep in the glade. It
came through the tops of the thinning trees where the
fringe of the jungle skirted the white sand. The patches of
sky there, were old lavender. They seemed glary, but that
was because my eyes had been accustomed to the
depressing darkness of the sunless swamps. Two days of
stumbling horror where every thorn that stung your legs
might be a bushmaster; where every cracking twig at night
might be a jaguar; where every bowing branch might be a
boa. The sky looked glorious.

You don't see the sky in the jungle. The trees are too
thickly grown together.

I was badly spent. I was too old for this sort of flight. I
knew well enough that, had it not been for Cambreau's
help most of the way, I should never have made it.

There were cruel scratches covering my legs, where the
brush had ripped my trouser legs to shreds. They stung
deeply and burned dully. My truss had slipped out of
place and though I kept pushing it back, it would not stay.
I felt that my hernia would come through. It kept me
coughing until I thought my lungs would explode. Half-
blind with nervous exhaustion I stumbled behind Cambreau, my hand on his left shoulder, until the white sand
of the beach sucked at my feet and pulled me down to it,
where I lay on my face, panting and coughing alternately.

Cambreau knelt down beside me, but did not look at
me. He stared into the west and I heard him sigh.

I was sick. The reaction had left me in awful shape. My
chest heaved, filling my throat with sour-tasting phlegm.

9

In the pit of my stomach was a high sense of nausea, which did not materialize. It was a miserable sensation. I wanted to vomit and get it over with, but nothing came. I couldn't see anything at all – only a blur of sand in front of me. I lay there, collapsed, my cheek resting on my sweating forearm as the dull throb of my heart filled my ears. The beach was so still, I fancied for an instant that even Cambreau could hear it. It boomed. . . .

A long time later, when I had regained my breath a little, I felt that Cambreau was staring at me and turned to see that he was. He smiled at me and said: 'Doctor, you must see this. You must not miss it.'

I asked hoarsely: 'What is it?' When I spoke the phlegm rattled in the back of my throat, and I coughed *hagh hagh* until it hurt my groin.

'The sky,' he said. 'You must watch the sky.'

I looked at the sky. In the west, beneath a still small cloud, there was a purple bruise as though the sun had struck the sky in passing. In the east, sweeping at us out of Africa, a grey curtain slowly dropped. In the north the cold stretches of intergalactic space had turned into deep blue. I didn't look south. I never wanted to look south again.

Hell lay south of the sixth parallel – St. Pierre. There was no beauty back there. In one glance you saw the copper of the Maroni's waters, the agonized green of the fecund forest, the bloody red of the clay banks, the stark white of the stuccoed houses, the pinpoint azure of the cloudless sky, the murky brown of the ominous buzzards. Nothing yelled. Nothing was congruous. The colours hurt.

I didn't speak for some time, but lay watching the sky. The nausea stayed with me. My glasses bothered me, too. I took them off; the ear-catch on the left side was bent. I tried to straighten it, but the tensile strength of the wire was gone and I could do nothing with it. I put the glasses on and lay down on my back again.

10

The coughing wouldn't leave me, and every time I coughed I'd get little pains stabbing the back of my head. There was a queer sensation inside, as though my brain had shaken itself loose and was sloshing around crazily.

It was no good on my back. I sat up. The coughing stopped a little. I looked at my legs and winced when I saw the scratches. My leg muscles were knotted hard as rock. I massaged them a little. It didn't do any good.

After a while Cambreau got up and walked down to the sea where it licked the beach about twenty feet away. I saw him strip off his shirt and fold it in his hand. He waded out a few feet, dipped it into the water, then came back and handed it to me.

I said: 'What's this for?'

'I thought you might like to wash your face.'

'Thank you,' I said. I took the shirt and wiped my face with it. The water was cold. It felt good. While I was using his shirt, Cambreau went back to the beach and took off his trousers. He folded them neatly and laid them on the sand. Then he walked into the water again. He didn't hesitate at all, just kept wading until it was deep enough for him to swim. I frowned and called: 'Be careful there! The barracuda come in close to shore.'

I heard him laugh and he swam eastward, disregarding the warning. Shrugging, I took his shirt and rubbed it over my legs. The salt stung the cuts and made me grit my teeth. But it was good for me. Antiseptic.

In a few minutes it had grown so dark that I could no longer see Cambreau as he swam. There was no moon. The sea was placid. I could follow the green line of foam where the shallow waves struck the beach. Listening for Cambreau's stroke in the water, I heard nothing.

I began to feel worried. But suddenly he was standing beside me again, his trousers back on his hips. He said: 'Hello! Did you watch me?'

I said: 'You shouldn't have done that. The barracuda come way in on this coast. They'd tear you to ribbons in a

11

minute. Sharks too. It's not safe to wade in even up to your knees.'

'Doctor,' he said reproachfully, 'sharks can't swim in two feet of water. You must know that.'

'Small barracuda can,' I said.

He smiled and sat down beside me. 'Don't worry. If I leave the barracuda alone, the barracuda will leave me alone.'

'Your shirt is there beside you,' I said. 'Thank you for it. I'm quite refreshed.'

He picked it up and put it on slowly.

'Did I get sand on it?' I asked. 'I'm sorry.'

'It's all right,' he said.

I said: 'Isn't this breeze fine? It came with the darkness. I haven't felt a cool breeze in months.'

'I hadn't noticed,' he said.

'That's right,' I said. 'You've been swimming. It must have refreshed you.'

'I didn't go swimming to be refreshed,' he said. 'I wasn't tired.'

'What do you mean by that?' I asked.

'I wasn't tired.'

'You weren't tired after to-day?'

'No.'

I said: 'And I suppose you aren't hungry either.'

'No,' he said.

'Well, I am,' I said irritably. His serenity annoyed me. 'I'm tired and I'm hungry and I feel rotten.'

'I don't,' he said.

'How are your legs?' I asked. 'Badly scratched?'

'I hadn't noticed,' he said. 'Not particularly.'

'Oh, for God's sake,' I said.

There was a long silence after that. We just sat there and watched the phosphorescence where the waves broke. My glasses felt loose again. I reached up and tried to tighten the catch on the left ear but it didn't do any good.

12

Cambreau said suddenly: 'One day, Doctor, you're going to feel foolish at having worn those things so long and you'll stop using them.'

'That will be nice,' I said. 'And I suppose I'll feel foolish at having worn this other thing and I'll throw that away too and have a strangulated hernia.' I sighed. 'You're talking nonsense.'

We sat and peered into the darkness. I asked: 'Is this the right place I wonder? Moll said a beach with white sand.'

'Nine miles west of us,' Cambreau said, 'is Iracoubo. Matacacao should be east of us, about five miles. This is the only white beach between those two points.' He paused. 'This is the one Moll meant, I think.'

'Then the boat –'

'The boat should be half a mile or so east of us. The beach curves out like a finger at that point and Gruno has left a rock cairn on the sand at right-angles with the hiding-place.'

I glanced at him sharply. 'How do you know that?'

'Oh,' he answered, 'I must have heard Gruno tell Moll.'

'Well,' I said, 'thank God anyway. We're here. That's something. That's more than half of it. We won't be bothered by any land patrols. They don't come over this far. We've only the sea patrols to escape now.'

'The sea patrols don't come this far east,' Cambreau said.

'How do you know?'

He didn't answer. I had a distinct impression that he was laughing at me in the darkness. Mild anger pervaded me. I said shortly: 'I'm going to try and sleep. You do as you wish.' I turned on my right side and curled up my knees, resting my cheek on the crook of my elbow.

'By the way,' he said, after a brief quiet, 'do you know what kind of boat Gruno has left for us?'

'No,' I said.

'Probably a sloop,' he said, musing. 'Yes, a sloop, I'm

13

sure. That would do nicely; say about twenty-two feet stem to stern. . . . Yes, a sloop would do. . . .'

'So would an ocean liner,' I said, still annoyed. 'Good night.'

4

I must have slept for a long time because when I awakened there was a full moon high in the sky, and the beach was clearly illuminated.

One moment I had been sound asleep. The next, wide-awake. Vaguely disturbed I rubbed my eyes and sat up. I wondered what had startled me. Perhaps Cambreau had touched me, I thought, and I glanced over to see if he had.

He wasn't there.

I stared at the cradled spot in the sand where he had lain and I felt anxious. Where had he gone?

Then I heard a dull kind of crunching. Or maybe I felt it first in my hands. They were resting on the sand. I looked up and down the beach – and I could see very far in the moonlight – but there was no sign of anyone. I leaned down and pressed my ear against the sand. Sure enough. Some one was walking on the beach. I could hear each footfall plainly, and then a squishing sound, as though something were dragging.

'Doctor.'

I jerked up, startled, and found Cambreau beside me.

'Hello,' he said.

'Where did you come from?' I said. 'You weren't here a second ago.'

'You shouldn't be frightened,' he said. 'Don't ever be frightened of me.'

'Where did you go?' I asked impatiently.

'I went down the beach. I knew that Moll would be arriving. I felt that he might need help – even if it won't do him any good, now.'

I said: 'What are you talking about?'

'I tried to drag him up here,' he went on, 'but it was too far. I think it would be better if we went to him instead.'

'Is Moll really here?' I asked.

'Of course he's here,' Cambreau said. 'He's been here for the last ten minutes, a hundred yards down the beach.'

'What's the matter with him?'

'He's dying,' Cambreau said.

'Dying!' I rose to my feet as quickly as I could. 'What are you talking about?' I felt dazed and thick-witted.

'I think you'd better come along,' Cambreau said. 'He's in pain and you may be able to help him, though I don't think you'll be able to save him. He's been bitten in the ankle.'

'Bitten!' I said sharply. 'By a snake?'

'A fer-de-lance,' he said as we hurried down the beach. 'It must have struck him just as he left the jungle for the beach.'

'Good God!' I said. 'He's got to live! He can't die now!'

'He won't die now,' Cambreau replied. 'But he's not going to live. I can tell you that.'

'But the escape –' I said. Then we reached him.

He was lying on his back, his face upturned to the moonlight. His skin was dead-white in the glow. His eyes were closed and although he groaned and writhed I think he was unconscious. I looked at his pupils, but there wasn't enough light to see them distinctly. I felt his forehead. It was icy. My hand came away wet with perspiration. It ran down his cheeks like water. His nose and his mouth were bleeding slightly. His respiration was good. His pulse was good.

I took a look at his right leg. It was swelling perceptibly, filling out his trouser leg – the cloth was almost taut. I said: 'I need a knife to cut this thing. I'll need a knife to lance the wound too.'

'I haven't a knife,' Cambreau said.

I felt Moll's pockets and found some matches, a cheap

little compass, the battered Bible, a map, but no knife.

'I've got to have a knife,' I said mechanically.

Cambreau turned and walked off towards the shore. I stared after him for a moment and then tried to rip the trouser leg. The cloth held tenaciously for a moment, and suddenly ripped apart, exposing the leg fully. It was pretty bad. Looked like a case of advanced septicemia, but of course it wasn't. The region around a venomous bite always swells. It was discoloured, boldly cyanotic, even in the moonlight. The ankle was huge. I took one of Moll's matches and struck it on the side of my trousers. When it lighted I held it down close to the ankle to examine the bite.

There were two bites. I could make out the twin fang marks in two different places. The first bite was just below the anterior side of the tibia. The second bite was directly above the ankle. I could tell this was the second bite because there was a fang still stuck in one of the wounds; the snake had bitten deeply. Moll's foot was dirty. There was swamp mud in between the toes.

I looked up to call Cambreau as the match went out, and found him standing beside me. He had a large shell in his hand, and as I watched he broke it in half and handed me a piece.

'This is very sharp,' he said. 'Even better than a knife. Use the broken edge and you will find it cuts cleanly.'

I felt the shell with my thumb and found it razor-edged.

'All right,' I said. 'I'm going to need help. You hold a match over the ankle while I cut.'

'All right,' Cambreau said.

He struck a match and held it while I poised the broken shell like a scalpel and went to work. I dug under the fang, lifted it, and flung it as far towards the fringe of the forest as I could. Cambreau watched with interest where it landed. The shell was better than I had hoped. I cut into the lower bite and sliced a canal between the two fang marks, from which blood instantly flowed. Then I crossed

17

that canal with another, running vertically between the fang marks. It made an *X* incision over the entire area. I did the same thing with the upper bite and soon the blood was flowing pretty freely, undoubtedly mixed with the excess venom in that region.

I tore off the sleeve of my shirt then, and picking up a dry stick, thrust it through the knotted piece of shirt and applied a tourniquet to Moll's leg above the knee.

I said: 'You hold this, Jean. Those wounds have got to be sucked. There's a lot of venom still there.'

'Your lips are chapped,' Cambreau said. 'They have open cuts. And there are scratches near your mouth.'

'What of it?' I asked.

'You'll get venom in your own system,' he said.

I said: 'That makes no difference. I've got to take the chance. We can't let him die. He's got a good chance of pulling through. His pulse is strong and his respiration is good.'

Cambreau shook his head slowly. 'Even anti-venim wouldn't save him.'

His manner irritated me. 'Hold the tourniquet!' I said sharply.

He stood there for a moment, paying no attention to me and staring at Moll. Then he went to his knees and said: 'You hold the tourniquet, Doctor.' And he bent over and applied his mouth to the wounds. He sucked out the flow and spat it on the sand until finally no more blood came.

I released the tourniquet for a few moments, to guard against gangrene, and then tightened it again. I said: 'That's enough. You won't get any more now. . . . Let's see how he does.'

Cambreau rose lightly to his feet. 'I still think he's going to die. He probably won't last past tomorrow night.'

I looked up at him. His face was very serious. He said: 'You did a fine job, anyway.'

5

About an hour later Jesus Telez, the sullen young Spaniard, came down the beach from the east, panting hotly and holding his shoulder. He plumped down beside us wearily and said: *'Buenas noches, señores.'*

His clothes were in tatters and his face and legs were badly scratched. The moonlight glistened on the crucifix around his throat. He thought Moll was asleep until he saw the ankle. Then he gasped and said: *'Dios mio, que es?'*

'It's Moll,' I said.

'Si, si, pero la pierna . . .'

'He's been bitten by a snake,' I said.

Telez looked horrified. *'Barba amarilla?'*

'Yes,' I said.

He crossed himself and tightened his mouth. Cambreau sat directly opposite him and regarded him curiously, smiling faintly as he saw the golden crucifix. I took the tourniquet off Moll's leg and kept it off. He had stopped sweating. He had stopped his empty retching too. Pulse: good; respiration: good.

We sat there silently and watched him.

Presently I dozed. When I awakened both Telez and Cambreau had disappeared. I quickly sat up, concerned, and looked about me. The moon made the sea a spread of sparkles. . . .

I wanted to go and look for them but I couldn't leave Moll. I examined the ankle and found the wound clean, with irrigation excellent. I felt his brow. It was hot now. He breathed very regularly. He had stopped groaning. He was still unconscious.

A few minutes afterward I saw the shadow of a man against the reflection of the moon on the sea, and as I watched it grew larger, approaching me. I said warily: 'Hello. Who's there?'

'Telez.'

When he reached me he squatted on the sand and buttoned up his trousers, keeping his eyes down on the sand away from the vicinity of Moll's ankle. His lips were suddenly tightened. Every now and then he winced.

I asked: 'Where did you go?'

He nodded his head at the water. 'Washed.'

'You shouldn't do that,' I said, taking my hand and placing it on his shoulder. 'Don't go out far.'

'Aow,' he said, and fell away from me.

I stared at him. 'What's wrong with you?'

'Nothing,' Telez said.

'Then why did you cry out?' I asked. 'It's your shoulder.'

'It's nothing,' he said. 'Leave me alone. It's nothing at all.' He spoke in Spanish.

'It's your shoulder,' I said.

'No.'

'That's why you washed,' I said. 'You were washing your shoulder.' I grabbed him by his good arm and pulled him towards me. He wouldn't come. He snapped his wrist away and glowered at me. I could see a dark patch on the left shoulder of his shirt. 'Be sensible, Jesus. I'll fix it for you. What happened?'

'Don't call me Jesus,' he said sullenly. 'Leave me alone. It's nothing.'

I started to reply when I glanced around and found Cambreau back again, sitting on the far side of Moll.

I asked: 'Where were you?'

'I was looking for the snake,' he said.

'The snake? . . . What snake?'

'The snake that bit Moll,' Cambreau said.

'For God's sake, must you do that? Do you want to be

bitten too? We've enough on our hands with Moll. I'm glad you didn't find it.'

'I did,' he said.

My heart jumped. 'Where?'

'Oh, down there. . . .' He motioned with his hand.

'It didn't –'

He smiled and shook his head, then looked at Telez and frowned. He asked: 'Aren't you afraid to go into the sea with the barracuda and sharks as omnivorous as Dr. LaSalle says they are?'

'There is also God,' Telez said in Spanish. He said it hurriedly and sharply and he avoided Cambreau's face.

Cambreau turned to me. 'Did you examine his wound?'

I said: 'What wound?'

'The gash in his shoulder,' Cambreau said. 'I saw him washing it.'

I wheeled to Telez. 'Let me see it. I knew something was wrong with your shoulder.'

Telez's eyes were wider than usual. He watched Cambreau steadily as he said to me: 'Leave me alone. I am all right. It is nothing. Just leave me alone.'

'How did you cut yourself?' I asked.

Telez said: 'That man is a devil.' He was still looking at Cambreau.

I ignored him and said again: 'Let me see your shoulder. How did you hurt it?'

'Maybe Verne gave it to him,' Cambreau said.

Telez's jaw dropped. *Es un diablo, Dios mio, es un diablo!*

He turned on me savagely. 'For the love of Christ, leave me alone.'

I looked at Cambreau.

'But . . . how could Verne have . . .' I stopped, aghast. 'You mean you think he is on his way here?'

'Ask Jesus,' Cambreau said.

'Don't call me that! Don't you call me that!' Telez said hostilely.

21

I said: 'Is it true? Telez! Is Verne on the way? Did he stab you? And where is DuFond? You were with DuFond. You were supposed to stay with him. Where have you left him?'

'Leave me alone!'

'No. You've got to tell us.'

'Ah . . .' Telez sighed and dropped his head into his hands. '*Si*. Verne is coming. *El parasito!*'

'How did he know? . . .'

'He watched DuFond,' Telez said. 'When DuFond left St. Pierre with me, Verne followed us. Last night he caught up with us when we camped.'

'What happened?'

'He said that he was going to come along in the boat. I told him that he could not come because he had not paid his share – and that we did not want him.'

'And then?'

'Then he said that he was coming along and if Moll didn't like it he would kill Moll.'

'He won't kill Moll,' Cambreau said softly. 'Moll will be dead all by himself. Look at him.'

Telez moved away from Cambreau uneasily. Moll was breathing heavily but he looked no worse.

I asked: 'What happened then?'

'Then . . . I hit him. I hit him in the face.'

'Why did you do that?'

Telez turned away. 'He called me a son of a bitch, so I hit him. I wish I had killed him. *El perro peludo!*'

I asked: 'How did he stab you?'

'He grabbed my own knife,' Telez said. 'But I got it back again. I cut him too. In the arm. Then I ran. I walked half the night.'

I asked: 'What did DuFond do?'

Telez shrugged. . . . 'He is afraid of Verne.' He fingered his shoulder. 'But I'm not. I will kill him yet.'

'Listen to me,' I said to Telez. 'Did he – did Verne and DuFond. . . .'

22

Telez shook his head. 'He has a woman with him. A black. She is a prostitute from the river. He left DuFond alone. He tells the woman that he is going to take her to America. That's all. Now leave me alone.'

We sat in silence again, a long time. Moll's breathing was a little hoarse, and irregular. It worried me. The swelling was about the same. His pulse was pretty strong. After a while I fingered the things I had taken from his pocket. I put the matches away, and tried to scan the map; but the moon was waning and I could not make it out. I folded it and put it in my pocket. Then I looked at the compass, but it was too dark to see the needle. I put that away too. I felt around for the old Bible, but I couldn't find it. I muttered: 'That's queer,' and kept groping in the sand.

'I have it,' said Cambreau.

'You have what?' I asked.

'What you're looking for.'

'Then give it to me,' I said. 'It's not yours. It's Moll's. I'll keep it with his things.'

He pulled the bible out of his trouser pocket and handed it to me.

'You ought to read it,' he said to me; then, 'Moll won't want it any more.'

Telez moved back a trifle farther. 'That man is a devil,' he said harshly.

I trembled a little and laid the Bible down beside me. I took a deep breath and then I asked Cambreau: 'Are you a devil?'

Cambreau looked surprised. 'Why do you ask that, Doctor?'

I said: 'You seem – well, queer. And then you anticipate things.'

There was a long silence. 'Well . . .' he asked, 'why a devil? Why not an angel? . . . Angels can anticipate things, can't they?'

I shivered and asked: 'Who are you, anyway, Jean?'

23

'A devil!' Telez said again.

Cambreau sighed. 'Never mind. One day you may see me as I am.' I watched him, still shivering. He rose to his feet and considered me thoughtfully. At last he smiled.

'Flaubert may be along soon,' he said. 'Don't be frightened when you see him. He's sure to be upset.'

He went westward down the beach and disappeared in the shadows.

6

Flaubert did come along.

I had slept soundly and when I wakened I was cold as ice and there were goose-pimples all over me. The scratches were biting, too. For a second, I thought that was what had awakened me; but it wasn't. I looked around and saw that Moll was still unconscious. Telez asleep, Cambreau not back yet. Then I heard a voice:

'Dr LaSalle!'

The cry emanated from the darkness of the jungle, still visible in the fading moonlight. It was husky and terrified; I shuddered as I jerked over on my side, my eyes widened, my breath spasmodic. A long probing pain stabbed up from my groin. I said apprehensively, almost inaudible from the sudden awakening: 'Who's there? Who is it?'

'It's I, Doctor! Poor Rudolph! Save me, Doctor! He's going to kill me! He's after me and he's going to kill me, just like he killed Dunning!'

'Flaubert,' I said, half to myself. 'The one they called insane.' I rose to my feet and peered at the place where the black woods and white sand met. 'Where are you? I don't see you.'

Slowly Flaubert raised his head above the bush behind which he was hidden. A ray of moonlight struck the top of his head and gave him an eerie colour. The effect was macabre. His rounded skull, completely devoid of hair, gleamed whitely. I could make out his eyes, staring and glassy, widened in horror. He said: 'Here I am, Doctor! . . . Poor, poor Rudolph!'

I hardly heard him. I heard instead Moll's laboured

breathing and instantly stiffened, thinking of the fer-de-lance which had struck his leg. I called fervently: 'Come out of that bush, Flaubert! For God's sake, come out of that bush on to the sand!'

He had been waiting for that, apparently, for he plunged through the bush and stumbled blindly across the sand. When he reached me he fell towards me and caught me around the knees, knocking me down. I was hurt again. I half-scrambled back, thinking for the moment that he had brought me down in attack; but soon I felt him grovelling at my feet, saying: 'You'll save me, won't you? You'll save poor Rudolph? You won't let him hurt me, will you?'

I felt sorry for him. I sat up and patted his hand and said gently: 'Of course I won't let him hurt you, Flaubert.'

He stopped grovelling and started to cry. He really wept, screwing his face up piteously, his lower lip bending down like a stretched bow. The tears fell into the sand and rolled themselves into small balls of dust.

I patted his hand. 'Don't do that,' I said. 'You're going to be all right now.'

'He was going to kill me,' he said, sobbing.

I asked: 'Who?'

'Weiner,' he said. He brushed his eyes with the backs of his wrists. The crying ceased abruptly and his eyes narrowed as he glared at me. 'You won't let him?'

'No,' I said. Weiner was the German with the 'leader' complex.

Flaubert leaned towards me, suspicious, and said in an even, almost menacing undertone: 'Don't you lie to me!'

'I wouldn't lie to you, Flaubert,' I said; and added in a flattering tone, '*You* know that.'

'Yes,' he said, his eyes saddening. 'I know it. . . . It was Weiner. All the time in the jungle I could see he was going to kill me. And maybe Dunning was too. Oh, they didn't want me along with them. They said: You're crazy, Flaubert, get the hell out of here. – They kept saying that

26

when all the time they knew I wasn't crazy at all.'

I stared at him. 'Did you say Dunning was dead?'

'I'm not crazy,' he said. 'I'm not crazy at all, am I, Doctor?'

'No,' I said. 'What about Dunning?'

'He's dead,' Flaubert's eyes blazed. 'Weiner killed him!'

'How do you know; did you see it?'

'This morning,' he said, pulling down his brows, 'I saw him there cold and stiff lying on his back. I said to Weiner, 'I'll tell on you, I'll tell about this, you murderer. You'll murder me soon if I don't. You're a murderer.' And he said, 'I ought to murder you, by God. I'd be doing the world a favour getting it rid of a lunatic like you, damn you. Get away from me.' Then I ran away from him and I ran all day. . . . I'm so tired. Poor Rudolph, he's so tired. Poor, poor Rudolph. . . .'

I patted his head. 'Poor Rudolph, your head is so hot –'

He flared up like a match. 'It's not hot! It's not hot at all! You can't say I'm crazy, either. I'm as sane as you are!'

I said: 'I know you are.'

'Then don't pity me. Don't touch me. My head's not hot!' He jerked away, went off a few feet and lay down on the sand, muttering to himself. I watched him anxiously for a while. He finally stretched out and stared up at the stars. His lips moved soundlessly, and at intervals one or two words came out. I heard: '. . . Poor Rudolph!' once more; and just before he dropped off to sleep he cried: '. . . no, Mary, no . . .'

Then the beach was silent again: silent of human talk, that is, for there was always the murmuring surf and the whispers of the trees in the forest behind the beach. And there was Moll's erratic breathing and Telez's healthy snoring and behind it all the silent roar of the black vastness of space which stretched out before us.

7

Once I dreamed I awakened. When I opened my eyes (as I thought) there was Cambreau on the other side of Moll and he smiled at me and said: 'Hello!' as though he had never seen me before.

I said: 'Hello,' and watched what he was doing.

The moon had vanished and it was very dark but I could see him plainly. That was the odd thing. It bothered me, in my dream, being able to see everything so clearly when it was dark.

Around Cambreau's right arm was coiled a mottled fer-de-lance with its yellow throat raised up and all aglow. The snake had lifted its head towards his face. Its jaws were closed and on the right side of the mouth a thin line of blood trickled down. Cambreau had a piece of his shirt in his free hand. The piece was wet. He reached over and wiped away the blood on the side of the snake's mouth.

I said: 'What are you doing?'

'I'm cleaning his mouth,' he said. 'It's bleeding where he lost that fang.'

'Is that the snake that bit Moll?' I asked.

'Yes,' he said. 'Isn't he a beauty?'

'For God's sake,' I said, 'put him down before he bites you too.'

'He won't bite me,' Cambreau said.

'Put him down!'

'He won't bite me,' he said. 'But don't you come near him. If you're afraid of him he'll strike you. He can sense fear. He can sense hate too. Go back to sleep, Doctor.'

So, in my dream, I went back to sleep.

The next time I opened my eyes I found that I was really awake, and the sun – coloured like the meat of a ripe plum – was shooting up in the east.

8

Telex was shaking me and saying: '*Levantese usted, levantese usted*. Moll is conscious.'

I got up and slipped my truss into place. It itched on the hips. The thing had been on continuously for three days now and the heat and sweat had made the leather irritate the flesh. I felt tired and stiff and sore. My legs ached.

Moll was groaning softly. His grey eyes were open. They couldn't focus. The irises were widely dilated and he just stared straight up at the slate sky with its first flush of dawn. His chin seemed to have fallen away from his upper jaw; his mouth was open and dragged down. His lips covered his teeth. He looked like an old, old man.

When I was wide awake I stooped down on the sand beside him and felt his pulse. It was still fairly strong, but losing ground. I didn't like the way he breathed. He inhaled with unnatural alacrity and his breaths were shallow, so that they made his chest just twitch instead of fill. There was cyanosis.

Telez was watching interestedly and I said to him: 'Tear off a piece of shirt, wet it and bring it to me.'

'*Si,*' he said and walked down to the water.

Moll's face was burning.

Presently Telez came back and handed me a piece of his shirt, soaking wet. I folded it without wringing out any of the water and washed Moll's face with it. It took off a surprising amount of sweaty dirt. He seemed to respond to its coldness; his pupils contracted slightly and he tried to turn, raising his left hand weakly and sweeping it towards me. I grasped it and put it back on his body. And then I noticed that his fingers were fluttering as though reaching for something.

That was a bad sign.

I said softly: 'Moll . . . Henry, can you hear me?'

He made no indication, but his bloodless lips moved rapidly. They were parched from fever. I leaned over to see if I could hear the words. None came out.

Telez said: *'La pierna . . .'* He shook his head.

The leg was in poor shape. It had swollen so much it looked unbelievable. I had cut the entire trouser leg up the side, of course – the expansion would have swelled it out and caused constriction under the thigh where the seam ran. The twin X incisions had stopped irrigating. They looked dirty. There was a foul odour from the wounds. The foot and ankle were black, the flesh beginning to wither. The shin and thigh were deep purple.

There was nothing to do.

I looked around. Cambreau was not there. Flaubert was sound asleep, his left cheek and the top of his hairless head were covered with sand. Telez was getting out of his trousers. I asked: 'What are you going to do?'

He said: *'Me lavo en el oceano.'*

I watched him and waited for him to take off his shirt so that I could see the wound in his shoulder. He sensed my purpose and didn't take it off. He had narrow hips and thin legs, with thick black hair on them.

I asked: 'Where's Cambreau?'

'No sé,' he said. 'He was gone when I awoke. I'm going to wash now. I'll be back soon.'

'Don't go out too far,' I said.

'Leave me alone,' he said.

'Don't be so irritable,' I said.

He went off without a word and waded into the sea up to his hips, then scrubbed his legs with his hands. While he was there he saw a man coming along the beach from the west. He waved to me and pointed west so that I would look.

31

It was Weiner, the irascible German, all alone. He was walking quickly, but apparently he was not tiring himself despite the retarding suck of the sand. His arms and face were scratched, and his trousers in ribbons, like Flaubert's. I could see his scratches easily. He came close quickly. I stood up and waved and said: 'Hello!'

He didn't wave back or answer until he reached me. Then he plumped down on the sand, panting a little, and regarded Moll with sour indifference.

'What the hell is the matter with him?' he asked, his voice surly.

'He was bitten by a snake,' I said. 'He's a sick man. It's touch and go with him.'

'Serves him God-damn right,' Weiner said. 'Making me go through that jungle with a crazy bug like poor Rudolph!'

I said: 'That's no thing to say.'

'I'm saying it,' he said sharply. 'You heard me. If you think it's been a picnic with that maniac, you're as crazy as he is. God almighty, you should have heard him! He yelled about poor Rudolph until I thought I'd go nuts! He gave me the creeps all the way.'

'Just the same,' I said, 'it's no thing to say about Moll. I think he's dying.'

Weiner shrugged. 'That's his hard luck. A man's a God-damn fool to run that jungle without antivenin, myself included.'

I thought of Cambreau: *Antivenin wouldn't save him.*

Weiner said: 'I see poor Rudolph got here all right. He would. Look at him, like a sleeping beauty. Some day, by God, the sovereign state will execute maniacs like him and rid society of them. When you have people like poor Rudie running around loose, free to breed, you can count on a bunch of imbeciles and morons and idiots and God knows what in your next generation. You've got to stop it by killing them. It's damn nonsense sticking them in asylums. Costs the state too much money to keep them

32

alive. . . . And why? In God's name will you tell me why they keep bugs like Rudie alive?' He stopped abruptly and glanced at the sea. 'Is that the Spaniard?'

'Yes,' I said shortly. I didn't like Weiner.

'Well, he made it too, huh? I thought DuFond was with him. God almighty, what a trip it's been. Damn Moll for sticking me with Rudie and that other corpse. Bad enough trying to make it myself but with those two – it's a wonder I'm here – at all!'

'Flaubert said you killed Dunning,' I said.

'He's a liar,' Weiner said in disgust. 'Killed Dunning! Nobody had to kill Dunning. He was ready to die when he left. The first day in the jungle killed him. I found him stiff as a bamboo in the morning, lying right where he went to sleep. Rudie said I killed him? . . . don't tell me you believed him! Believed a bug like that? Don't be a fool. But I tell you, by God, it was a joy to me when that imbecile lit out on his own. He kept yelling: You're going to kill me too, and then he ran. A good thing too, because I might have killed him at that if he'd kept on giving me the jitters like he was. He damn well ought to be dead. . . . What are you staring at?'

'Nothing,' I said.

'Well, don't stare at me like that or I'll break your jaw.'

I said evenly: 'You'll break nothing.'

'Oh, no?' he said.

'No,' I said. 'You talk too much. You didn't talk so much when Moll was on his feet.'

'I'm not afraid of Moll,' Weiner said, sneering. 'I'm not afraid of any man.'

I laughed shortly. 'You wouldn't say that if Moll were all right. You wouldn't talk back to him.'

'The hell with Moll,' he said, reddening. 'I'll talk back to you. You're as bad as Flaubert. You're no damn good either, and you know it.' He got up and went over to where Flaubert was still sleeping, despite the conversation. 'Look at him. Like a sleeping beauty. Get the hell up, Rudie, poor Rudie!' He kicked Flaubert savagely in the ribs.

Flaubert came out of his sleep wailing. It was instinctive to him. He leaped to his feet, stared at Weiner's laughing face a moment, then, uttered a shrill scream of terror and fled eastward along the shore. Weiner watched him until he reached the curve in the beach and disappeared.

I said: 'You wouldn't have done that if Moll were all right.' My voice was taut and raspy. 'You're a coward.'

His face leered. 'The hell with Moll. I'm not afraid of him. I never was afraid of him!' To prove this point he kicked Moll's prostrate body. Moll grunted but did not move. I stepped over and shoved him away.

'Leave him alone,' I said.

Weiner stared at me for a moment, then laughed heartily and gave me a push. I lost my balance and fell flat on my face. My truss slipped out of place and a long pain struck through me.

When I sat up Weiner was still laughing. Telez came back from the water and silently pulled on his trousers, eyeing Weiner coldly. Weiner said jeeringly: 'Well, well, hello. If it isn't little Jesus!'

Telez said nothing.

'Listen, you bandy-legged swine,' Weiner said, turning to me, shaking an index finger at my face; 'if you ever touch me again I'll break every bone in your body. You hear me? This crew is going to have a master, and I'm it, see? I'm the dictator. . . .' He paused and played with the word. 'Dictator . . . dictator. Sure, that's what I'm going to be! Dictator of the damned; and you'll do as I say.'

I said: 'All right. That's fine. You'll be dictator. You'll handle the whole escape.'

'Now you're talking,' Weiner said, surprised.

'Sure,' I said. 'I'm talking. It's going to be interesting. I want to see what you can do, you're always talking so much about the strong and the weak. Kill the weak. Raise the strong. That's Weiner sounding off. Weiner the

34

strong. I want to see how you handle us.'

'I'll handle you all right,' he said gratingly. 'You don't think so?'

'I'm not saying,' I said. 'But I want to see how you handle George Verne. Moll didn't want Verne along. Moll knew he couldn't handle Verne. All right. You're dictator. I want to see how *you* do it – how *you* handle Verne.'

Weiner looked blank. He wet his lips and looked at my eyes for a long time. Then he glanced over at Telez. Telez was buttoning his trousers. There was nothing in his face at all. He just had a sullen expression around his mouth. Finally Weiner asked: 'What are you talking about?'

I said: 'Verne,' and I smiled nastily.

'Verne . . .' Weiner said slowly. 'What's he got to do with this? He isn't in.'

'Yes he is,' I said. 'He's in all right. He's declared himself in. He followed Telez and DuFond and he's coming on with DuFond now. He'll be here soon. I was worried that he'd take charge. Now he won't. You're going to be dictator.'

Weiner's eyes wavered. He looked vague. 'I'm not afraid of Verne,' he said emptily. 'I'm not afraid of anyone.' But now he was talking at himself.

'That's fine,' I said. 'That takes care of Verne, then. We won't have to worry about him.'

'I'm not afraid of him,' Weiner repeated. But he didn't believe it himself, and he knew it.

9

About fifteen minutes later another man appeared on the beach around the bend in the east, and called to us. We all sat up and peered at him. The sun was higher now and I could feel the heat starting. There was no breeze at all and the ocean looked like blue glass far out, and green glass where the water was shallow. The blue sky was very close. It is always like that in the tropics. The nearer the equator you are, the closer to earth the sky is. When you go to the temperate zones the sky rises and grows hostile and cold.

The man who had called from the bend in the shore was Louis Benet – the rapist. I was surprised to see him. I had expected all the men to arrive at precisely the spot where Cambreau and I did. Of course they had not. Benet had come out of the jungle far down the beach. When I saw him, I instantly thought of Pennington – who had started with him – and wondered whether or not his diseased lungs had held out.

Benet waved to us when he realized that we saw him. He didn't come any closer, just waved, and I got the idea that he was waving for us to come east on the beach.

Weiner got up and said: 'He wants us to come. By God, I'll bet he's found the boat!'

I got up too. Benet waved once more and then ran back and disappeared out of sight around the bend. Weiner started at once, walking towards the spot where Benet had vanished.

I said: 'Wait a minute. You've got to help me with Moll. I can't carry him alone.'

Weiner half turned round. 'The hell with him.'

'You can't do that,' I said. 'You can't leave him here. He's dying.'

'And a good thing,' Weiner said. 'What in hell is the use of carting him along with us? If he's going to die, let him die.'

'I'm not going to leave him.'

Weiner spat on the ground. 'God damn him,' he said. 'Carry him yourself, then.' He walked off quickly.

I turned helplessly towards Moll and sat down on the sand beside him. His hands moved restlessly. The sand was growing hotter. Telez came over by me and stood there silently for a minute. Then he said: 'Let us carry him together, Doctor.'

'How can we,' I asked, 'with your shoulder?'

'Never mind my shoulder,' he said. 'I can manage.'

'All right,' I said.

I tightened my truss into place and bent down. I took Moll under the shoulders. Telez took him under the knees. We strained and picked him up. He was a heavy man, solidly heavy. I could feel the strain down deep and I saw Telez set his teeth as his shoulder pulled. I was afraid his wound might be pulled apart; the bleeding might start again. He said nothing. Moll groaned loudly as pain pervaded him, and he spoke a lot of words; but they were senselessly jumbled. His tongue couldn't co-ordinate with his thought.

We stumbled along the beach until we were blind with pain, Telez with his shoulder, I with my hernia and Moll, no doubt, with his leg. We had to stop. We halted abruptly and laid Moll down on the warming sand while we dropped alongside him, panting hotly, our shoulders bent.

My head was whirling and I felt a little sick.

'Hello!' some one said cheerfully.

I looked up. It was Cambreau. He had come up very silently.

'Isn't it a glorious day!' he said. His eyes were sparkling

and he was thoroughly alive. He made me feel better.

I said: 'We were carrying Moll to the boat. He's very heavy. . . .'

Cambreau looked first at Telez and then at me. 'This is a good thing you've been doing. Why do you spoil it?'

I didn't understand him.

He stooped down and picked Moll up in his arms, without even straining, so far as I could see. Moll made no sound at all. Telez and I got to our feet and stared at Moll lying in Cambreau's arms like that.

Cambreau said: 'Come on, the boat is ready.'

'Ready?' I said. 'You mean – afloat?'

'Of course,' he said. 'It's been afloat all the time. Gruno left her in the water with her centre-board-box grounded. He had a line strung from a tree on shore to her bowsprit. He had her covered with underbrush to disguise her. I took it all off. The supplies are in.' He smiled at me provocatively. 'It's a sloop, Doctor. A twenty-foot sloop.'

I didn't say anything.

When we reached the bend in the beach we could see the boat. The sails were furled. The mast was set far forward in an improvised step. It was a makeshift rig at best. It had a bowsprit held in place with stays on either side, and the mast stuck up like a naked tree. There was no deck. We all had to sit on the thwarts, resting our feet down on the floor-boards. The boat looked inhumanly small. 'Don't worry about its smallness,' Cambreau said to me suddenly, as though he had divined my thought. 'We'll get a larger one when we reach Port of Spain.'

'That would be fine,' I said dryly, 'except that we're not going to Port of Spain.'

He shrugged and said nothing.

When we reached the spot where the sloop was floating we found Pennington, the tubercular American professor, sitting on the sand beside the loud-mouthed Weiner and Benet. Poor Flaubert, quieted now from the kicks which

Weiner had given him, was stretched out on his back, his eyes closed, his hands playing nervously across his hairless head. He grunted to himself. Benet nodded at me, washing his hands together. He made me shudder. Weiner got up and came over to me. 'Well, you brought him,' he said grinning. I went past him and over to Pennington. I sat down beside Pennington and shook hands with him.

Cambreau did not look at us at all. He stepped into the sloop with Moll in his arms and laid him gently down forward. Moll seemed to be asleep. His breathing was shallower than before and he was quite pale. The ankle looked the same. The leg too.

Cambreau came back and stepped out on to the sand. Weiner went over to him, 'Listen, you,' he said coldly, 'I don't want him in the boat. He's dying and he's no God-damn good to anyone, not even himself. He won't last two hours and I don't want any corpse in that boat, you hear me?'

'Yes,' said Cambreau.

'Then take him out,' said Weiner. 'Take him the hell out and leave him on the beach. If he's got to die, he's got to die. There's no sense crowding the boat with a dying man. I'm head of this escape now. You take him out.'

Cambreau sighed. 'You shouldn't have kicked him,' he said.

'He won't last two hours.'

Cambreau's face looked serious. 'You shouldn't have kicked Flaubert either.'

'He's crazy.'

'You shouldn't have hurt Dr LaSalle either,' Cambreau said.

'He –' Weiner stopped. His face was flushed. He realized that he had been excusing himself. He stepped threateningly towards Cambreau. Cambreau waited quietly. Weiner hesitated. Then his impulse to violence lost momentum. He turned, walked back and sat down on the sand.

Cambreau smiled at him. 'Moll won't be in your way,' he said.

Soon after this there was a sharp cracking of branches behind us and young Jacques DuFond came out of the pseudo-darkness of the jungle. His skin was bright red with heat and exertion. He looked very tired. Behind him a buxom negress followed. She had a multi-coloured piece of crettone wrapped around her hips, and another piece, differently patterned, over her breasts. Only it wasn't over her breasts. It was only over one of them. The other hung over the top of the cloth because the cloth had been pulled out of place while she fought the branches of the low-hanging trees. She was rinsed with sweat and it made her blackness gleam like onyx. She didn't have any whites to her eyes; they were all red-veined from fatigue.

Behind her came George Verne.

10

Verne was a brute. When you looked at him full front you saw a long face, the end of it covered with a shaggy red beard. When you looked at his profile you saw that his face was as flat as a saucer, the nose blunt, indented below the bridge, the brows shaggy, like the beard, and just as red. He squinted narrowly, never opened his eyes fully. They were light blue. He had short red hair which stuck up like wire from his skull.

Not a tall man, he was built horizontally. He seemed as wide as three ordinary men, squat, like a frog, and with powerful shoulders. He could rip a new shirt merely by tightening the muscles in his back. His hands were fat, his fingers short.

He had been in the colony nine years, convicted of one of the most cold-blooded murders I had ever heard of, and every man who had known him during those nine years hated and dreaded him. Every man, that is, but Henry Moll. Moll had been afraid of no one. Nevertheless he avoided Verne. There was too much animal in Verne, vicious unthinking animal.

No one said a word as he stood there on the beach and looked at each one of us, slowly grinning to show his yellowed teeth, ridged with brown lines where the enamel had worn away.

Finally he spoke. 'Hello, you gutless devils. I guess you didn't expect George Verne, did you?' He waved his arm and I noticed a slight cut on the forearm; I glanced at Jesus Telez. His dark eyes were fixed on Verne thoughtfully, and his left hand went inside his shirt to finger the knife he had, held by his belt next to his skin.

'Where's Moll? I've got to see him,' Verne went on. Then, as no one answered, 'I'm askin': where is Moll?'

Nobody said a word.

Verne's voice became thunderous. It was basso profundo and came up from his heels with a volume which beat at our ear drums. 'Are you all tongue-tied? *Where's Moll?*'

Weiner got to his feet and walked over to Verne, hesitatingly. Verne glared at him and the red beard jumped. 'Weiner, ain't it?'

'Yes,' Weiner said. 'Hello, Verne. Moll's in the boat.'

'In the boat, is he!' Verne said. 'Well, tell him to climb the hell out and come over here. George Verne wants to see him.'

'He's dying,' Weiner said. 'He was bitten by a snake. I told LaSalle, by God, that he wasn't any good to anyone, but LaSalle carried him along just the same. Then that man –' he pointed to Cambreau who was standing by the stern of the boat, '– put him in the boat. I told him that Moll wouldn't last two hours but he put him in the boat just the same. I told him I didn't want a corpse in that boat, but he put him in there.'

'*You* told him, did you?' Verne said, grinning. 'And who the hell do you think you are, Weiner? Master of this boat? I guess you thought you were master, eh?'

Weiner flushed and looked afraid. 'I didn't know –'

'You didn't know George Verne was here, eh?'

'I thought –' Weiner was miserable.

'What'd you think?'

'I thought –'

Verne laughed harshly and struck Weiner across the face with his closed fist. It was a powerful blow and knocked him spinning to the sand where he hastily scrambled away from Verne and held his face. There was a welt on it, and tears in his eyes from the sting.

'Next time,' Verne said, 'don't think so much.'

He strode across the beach to the boat, pushed by

42

Cambreau and waded out to his knees so that he could look into the boat at the bow. He ran his eyes over Moll's body, finally staring at the ankle. He said: 'Ain't that pretty, ain't that a pretty sight? . . . Moll, you swine, how strong are you now?'

He remained staring a minute or two, then walked back to the rest of us on the beach.

'Listen!' he roared.

He watched us jerk, startled, and laughed uproariously.

'I'm headin' this escape,' he said then. 'And if there's any one of you that don't think so, let's hear it.'

Nobody answered him.

'I'm the boss,' he said. 'I'm the master, you got that?'

Some of us nodded.

'What I say goes,' Verne said. 'If I say toss Moll overboard, that goes. You got that?'

I said: 'You couldn't do that, Verne. You wouldn't throw him overboard. He's dying.'

Verne grinned at me. 'No? I'll throw anybody I damn please overboard. And that means you too, you pot-bellied quack!' He liked that. He liked the uneasiness in my eyes. He laughed again. 'But I ain't goin' to throw Moll overboard, Doc. Not me, I ain't.'

'I'm glad,' I said.

'You know what I'm goin' to do?' he asked.

'No.'

'I'm goin' to watch him,' he said evenly, narrowing his eyes and hunching his shoulders together. 'I'm goin' to watch him all the time he suffers, all the times he dies. Good God, but I'm goin' to enjoy watchin' him suffer!'

I felt the sun on my face. It was hot.

Suddenly Verne bellowed: 'What the hell are you all waitin' for? What in hell are you all gawkin' for, sittin' on your tails like a pack of God-damned ninnies?'

Nobody answered.

'Get up!' he said. 'Get to hell into that boat! There's only a ten franc reward if they take us by land. They won't

43

come after us here. If we're goin' t'get taken, it'll be by sea where it pays fifty. Get started and give them a chance!'

We scrambled to our feet and went hastily to the boat. Flaubert reached it first, whimpering. He climbed in and started forward, then saw Moll and sat down amidships. Benet went after him. He went forward, to just behind Moll.

Verne said: 'You! Sit up with Benet. Yes, you, you loony devil. Move up with him!'

Flaubert jumped ahead on to the thwart beside Benet.

'All right,' Verne said. 'You next, LaSalle. Sit right behind them with Pennington.'

I said: 'I ought to sit with Moll. He's dying.'

'You sit with Pennington or I'll –'

'All right,' I said. 'I'll sit with Pennington.' I climbed into the boat with Pennington, who coughed now and then and looked at Verne with sad eyes.

'And you,' Verne said coldly to Telez, 'you, little Jesus, you sit behind LaSalle right where I can see you. I got somethin' to talk to you about, ain't I?'

Telez's face was inscrutable. He climbed silently into the boat and sat on the thwart behind me.

'All right,' Verne said, 'You, Jacques, you sit next to the wop.'

DuFond nodded resignedly and climbed in beside Telez. Verne glanced at Cambreau. 'Who the hell are you?'

'Jean Cambreau.'

'I never saw you before.'

Cambreau did not answer.

Verne stared at him. 'All right. You get up forward with Moll and keep your mouth shut.' He turned on his heel and walked back across the beach towards the Negress. We all watched him. 'Get in that boat,' he said, 'and sit on the back seat with me.'

The Negress grinned, showing white teeth, and ran to

44

the boat. Verne followed beside her. When she got to the boat she stopped suddenly when she saw Cambreau.

It was astonishing. Shame seemed to suffuse her black face. She quickly pulled up her rag of cretonne and stuffed her breast down behind it. Verne watched her puzzledly, then glanced at Cambreau standing by the stern of the boat.

Verne said: 'Get in the boat. Get the hell in! I told you once to get in and you do as I say or I'll leave you behind.'

Cambreau raised his hand and pointed at the Negress. He said: 'She isn't coming, Verne.'

'What?' Verne roared.

'She isn't coming.'

'Are you tellin' me what she's going' to do?'

'Yes,' said Cambreau. 'She isn't coming.'

Verne cursed and strode over to Cambreau, his fists wadded like rocks. When he reached Cambreau he stopped, looked him straight in the eyes, and said: 'Say that again, you!'

'She isn't coming. And LaSalle had better sit with Moll.'

Verne trembled and the muscles in his arms tightened. Instinctively I screwed up my face and waited for the blow, deploring Cambreau's foolhardiness. None came. Verne didn't hit him. Verne didn't even raise his hand. He stared, his red beard hanging down as his lower jaw dropped. Cambreau began to smile. Finally he said: 'Why don't you hit me, Verne?'

'Christ!' Verne said. It was all he could say.

The Negress had run back on the beach and stumbled to the sand where she was whining, frightened.

'All right,' Cambreau said. 'Move up by Moll, Doctor.'

I climbed past Benet and took a seat on the narrow forward thwart.

'All right,' Cambreau repeated. He waded out into the water until it was up to his knees and then climbed over the gunwale and sat down on the other side of me, facing the stern. He commanded a view of the entire boat. Benet and Flaubert, first, each on opposite sides of the mast. Then Pennington and Weiner. Then Telez and DuFond.

Verne was standing on the sand. Cambreau nodded to him. 'You can shove off now. You're going to steer.'

Verne responded automatically. He stepped forward and pushed hard against the stern. The centre-board scraped on the sand, gradually sinking as the boat floated away. Hastily, Verne splashed into the water, climbed on to the stern seat, and gripped the tiller.

Weiner looked at him with derision in his eyes.

'Break out the oars,' said Cambreau cheerily. 'There'll be a wind this afternoon. We'll row until then. Benet and Flaubert and DuFond will row. Doctor, your compass. What is the destination?'

I said deeply: 'You should know.'

He smiled. 'All right. Got the compass? Set a course north-west by west and keep Verne informed in the steering.'

The sea was like a dead lake. We moved gently out over it, feeling the bite of the sun on our heads and the glare with which it struck our eyes from the water. The men rowed awkwardly and slowly. The oars splashed us once or twice. But we moved steadily out and kept moving until the lonely Negress on the shore became a blackened dot, still prone on the white sand.

Soon she disappeared entirely and became only a part of the white stretch of beach and waving green forest which lay astern in the distance.

11

Moll died with the twilight.

All day long I watched him, despairing as his breathing grew quicker and shallower and the fever seemed to burn his great body into a withered skeleton. I shaded his face from the sun, which had burned us badly until we were wise enough to roll down our shirt sleeves and shield our faces with torn strips of cloth.

There was evidence in Moll's condition of a neurotoxic reaction which I had not expected to find along with the usual violent haemotoxic reaction of the venom. This was clear from the manner in which his respiratory centre gradually became paralyzed.

In the afternoon when a breeze sprang up and we hoisted the mangy sails Gruno had left us, giving respite to the exhausted rowers – Moll regained consciousness.

It was a queer kind of consciousness, sharp and unnaturally strong. He seemed to regain his senses and breath completely, for a minute. He opened his grey eyes and the pupils were not dilated at all. He looked at me, smiled and said: 'Hello, LaSalle, how's the rotting eggshell?'

I said: 'I'm fine, Moll.' I felt sorry for him.

'What happened to me?' he asked.

'A snake bit you in the ankle,' I said.

'Oh,' he said. 'What kind?'

'A fer-de-lance.'

'Oh,' he said. He sighed. Then he dropped off again, his breathing seemed to stop, and I thought for a moment that he had died.

As the afternoon wore on the heat seemed to stimulate

Pennington. He lost his sickly pallor, his cheeks took on colour. He didn't mind the sun at all, though it nearly prostrated the rest of us. He sat up and chatted pleasantly.

'. . . Take the empty room. You say it is filled with space. Then fill it with anything, water, furniture. Where has your space gone when it is filled? Space is only a mirage. . . . Like time.' I could understand why he spoke of space. It was all around us, sun, heat, water, and space, space, space, as far as we could see. Nobody listened to him except Cambreau – who agreed heartily and seemed pleased when he referred to time as an illusion. Most of the day, however, Cambreau had sat very still beside me, looking ahead with interest at the reach of the ocean. He did not cover his head with strips of his shirt. Indeed, he did not seem to feel the heat, and the sun did not bother him.

Later, Moll opened his eyes again, and looked at Cambreau. 'No!' he said. 'No . . . not you . . . no! LaSalle, LaSalle!'

I said: 'Yes?'

'Take him away!' Moll said, frantic; 'take that man away from me!'

'He won't hurt you,' I said.

'Take him away!'

Cambreau leaned over and looked directly into Moll's eyes. 'I can never go away,' he said. 'You know how futile it is to ask that. You've been afraid of me all your life. You've evaded me all your life. You can't evade me now.'

I felt frightened.

'I know,' Moll said in a whisper. 'I know . . .' Again he dropped off and lay as though dead.

Gently we moved, rising and falling with the unbroken swells, heading northwest. The wind continued, gentle as the sea, and the bow made a white comb where it cut the water.

We ate our day's share of food – it was welcome too –

48

and we drank our day's share of water from the wooden keg. It was warm from the sun, but fresh and sweet.

When twilight finally touched the sky Moll opened his eyes for the last time and said: 'Cambreau?'

Cambreau leaned over him. 'Yes.'

'Cambreau, now I know who you are.'

'Of course you do,' Cambreau said. 'Are you afraid?'

Moll smiled wanly. 'How can I be afraid?'

'You know it is nothing?'

'I know,' Moll said.

'Are you afraid of me?' Cambreau asked.

'No,' Moll said. 'I should have known you years ago.'

Cambreau shook his head. 'You could have known me years ago,' he said. 'You didn't want to. You wouldn't recognize me.'

'I know,' Moll said. He sighed. 'LaSalle?'

'Yes, Moll, I'm right here.'

'Good man,' he said quietly. 'He is a good man, isn't he, Cambreau?'

'To everyone but himself,' Cambreau answered.

'LaSalle?'

'Yes, Moll?'

'LaSalle,' he said, 'forgive me. I'm sorry for everything I ever did or said which hurt you.'

'That's all right,' I said. 'Forget that. Are you – have you any pain?'

'Oh, no,' he said. 'No pain at all.' He smiled just like Cambreau.

I said fervently: 'Moll, tell me, please tell me, who is he? Who is Cambreau?'

He closed his eyes, and murmured: 'God save me. . . .'

It was still light enough to see his face turn blue. His breathing grew hoarse and loud and gaspy, then it came in huge violent gulps. The inhalations became farther and farther apart until the last one came, jerking his body roughly. He turned white. I touched his chest, and the air hissed out of his lungs audibly. All in the boat heard it.

49

Telez crossed himself and mumbled a prayer. I felt for Moll's pulse.

'No need of that,' Cambreau said.

'He's dead,' I said.

We buried him a few minutes later. There was nothing to weight his feet down so we just had to push him overboard. It was dark enough not to be able to see him clearly. I was glad. . . . There was the splash, the drops of water in my face, then circles which spread out quickly.

I saw no sharks.

Later, I thought of the battered Bible which Moll had loved to mock. I had left it on the sand when Telez and I carried him east to the boat. I felt badly about it.

'I have Moll's Bible here,' Cambreau said suddenly. 'It is for you, later.'

'You have it?' I said. 'Did you find it on the beach?'

'Yes,' he said.

'Poor Moll. Did you hear what he said when he died. . . . "God save me". He was an atheist, you know.'

'Atheist is such an empty word,' Cambreau said.

'It is, isn't it?' I agreed. 'Still, it's queer he should have said "God save me" after all those years. . . . His last words.'

'That's always the way,' Cambreau said. 'God always gets the last chance.'

There was no word from Verne about Moll. It surprised me. He had spat over the side when we dumped the body, said: 'That's that,' and nothing more.

The sloop was heavily silent for a while. The only one who spoke was Flaubert. He cried softly and kept saying: '. . . Poor, poor Rudolph. . . . '

He was still repeating it when the moon rose and I fell asleep.

12

I dreamed again that night. I dreamed that I awakened and found the wind had died. There was no breath of wind at all, yet the sloop moved forward easily and steadily. I looked around for Cambreau and could not find him.

Then I saw him. Somehow it didn't surprise me. He was out in front of the sloop, walking across the sea and pulling us after him, holding a rope which stretched from the bowsprit of the sloop to his own shoulder.

He saw me looking at him and waved for me to come out and help him. I climbed over the gunwale and stepped across the water to him and took hold of the rope pulling. I could not feel the sea at all, could not feel its solidness nor its liquidness. I felt as though I had left my body behind me altogether. We pulled the boat easily. It had no weight at all. I said to him:

'What are you doing out here?'

'Pulling the boat,' he said.

'I know. But why?'

'To progress,' he said. 'The wind died tonight and the boat was becalmed. It stood still. Stagnation is the foundation of retrogression. Nothing should ever retrogress. We must progress. That is man's heritage – to go forward.'

'But the sloop is not a man,' I said.

'There are men in it,' he said.

Then it all faded and I awoke, sweating, cold, and shivery. This was the second dream of Cambreau I had had in two consecutive nights and I felt frightened. I turned and looked over my shoulder. Cambreau was sitting erect and still, staring up at the stars.

'Hello,' I said.

'Hello,' he said. 'It's a lovely night.'

'I just had a dream about you,' I said. 'An impossible thing!'

'Why impossible?' he asked.

I did not answer.

The wind was still with us. There was the sound of the water at the bow and the dry creak of the mast as our sails billowed.

13

The second day the wind held up nicely. It was a fresh breeze, steady and hot, and it kept us moving northward with white water at our bow.

When I awoke it was already stifling. There was evidently going to be no relief from the heat. It stayed with the night and then, just when it began to cool, the sun came up again and blazed away. I looked around the horizon and saw the sea and the sky. The sea was slate-coloured, not blue as it had been. The swells were deeper, more numerous. In the northeast dark clouds gathered.

We ate our rations of food and drank our ration of water. There was no cup and we had only one way to measure each man's water. We passed the keg and each of us took two swallows, filling his mouth with twice as much as it would hold. That was fair enough – anyway, it was all we could do.

The men were restless. The sun was hard to bear. Flaubert's poor hairless head was flaming, and water from beneath his skin had settled down over his eyes, making him limply bettle-browed. It must have been painful; he whimpered almost constantly.

Weiner's nose was burned. It looked like a tulip. He shielded it tenderly. His discomfort had made him even nastier than usual, and that, coupled with Verne's bald submission to Cambreau on the previous day, gave him an exaggerated sense of importance which he exercised constantly. Nobody listened to him. He took it out on Flaubert.

Benet, already deeply tanned from the sun at the colony, grew still darker. His olive skin could not have burned. It was too well protected by oil. He fairly shone with it. He did not talk at all, just squirmed restlessly.

Telez's dark skin protected him too from the scorching glare. But DuFond was beaten down. He was naturally light, and the sun played havoc with him. He looked broiled, despite the fact that he had covered himself. The reflection from the water had got him. He sat nearest the stern beside Telez, his head miserably in his hands. He swayed to and fro with the transverse roll of the boat, looking as though he were seasick.

Pennington, on the other hand, bloomed. 'I never felt so well in my life,' he said. 'Truly, Doctor, this is miraculous. I must come out here often. Did you notice that I had stopped coughing? I feel strong, really vigorous. This is glorious.' He looked healthy. He had bright glowing spots on his cheeks and a light in his mild eyes.

Verne had come out of his strange dormancy. I thought that he had been too inactive. Cambreau might have frightened him, but, knowing Verne, I realized it could not last. He had been squatting frog-like in the stern, his hand gripping the tiller, his red beard flowing with the breeze, his eyes squinted narrowly, always on Cambreau's back. But now they had switched, and that disturbed me. He seemed to have lost thought for Cambreau and now watched DuFond. There was perturbation in his expression, mingling with desire.
. . .

We met the swell adequately, riding swiftly down the slope of each comber into the placid valley at the bottom, there to plunge gently in with our bow and rise slowly up the opposite side and over the next crest. It was monotonous, yet soothing. There was no effort at all. The sloop was very seaworthy.

Weiner took voice now, and began to bellyache loudly. 'This God-damn heat is enough to broil a man alive. You could serve me on a platter, by God!'

54

I said: 'Forget it. Complaining isn't going to do any good.'

'You shut your damn mouth,' Weiner said. 'I'll say whether it's going to do any good or not. If I want to talk, I'll talk. I say it's hot. Hell couldn't be hotter than this. . . . How about it, Rudie poor Rudie?' He leaned forward and slapped Flaubert briskly on the top of the skull.

Flaubert stiffened as agony swept through him. His head was in rotten shape and no strength had been spared in the slap. For several seconds he struggled to scream, but pain choked his throat. I could see tears well up, break over his lower lids and stream down his face. Inwardly I was cold and steely. I could feel everything he felt.

At last he shrieked and broke the trance. The cry seemed empty against the sea.

Weiner looked startled at the sound and then began to laugh. He laughed heartily and slapped his legs. 'Rudie got a shock! Poor Rudie got the God-damndest shock of his young life. This is good! Why didn't I think of it before.'

Flaubert was terrified. He didn't know how to escape.

Leaning forward, still laughing, Weiner raised his hand to slap the glowing skull again.

Flaubert watched in fascination, his eyes riveted until the hand started down. Then he shrieked again, more loudly and shrilly, and jumped away towards the bow of the sloop, rocking us dangerously and sending up a frightened string of protests from the others.

Cambreau grabbed him; he struggled like a maniac, and Verne bellowed curses from the stern.

'What the hell is this? Sit down, you loony, sit down! What's the matter with him?'

'Weiner hit him on the head,' I said.

'Oh, God,' Weiner laughed. 'this is good!'

'Weiner,' Verne said, 'you shut that gapin' trap of yours or I'll bash your brains in!'

55

Weiner stopped laughing and sat motionless. Slowly he turned around and glared at Verne. Verne's hand was on the tiller. It was practically impossible for him to leave his post, come forward, attack Weiner and still keep the sloop afloat. Weiner grinned nastily. 'You go to hell,' he said.

Verne's face went purple. 'What?'

'You go to hell. Go to hell!'

The red beard twitched as Verne set his mouth murderously. 'Weiner,' he said hoarsely, 'when we reach port I'm going to beat you. I'm going to beat you till you can't see no more. I'm goin' to beat you till you're sorry you ain't dead.'

Weiner hadn't thought of that. He hadn't stopped to think that Verne could hurt him when we landed. He considered the possibility thoughtfully. He cast down his eyes and surveyed the floor-boards absently. He didn't like it. He stopped laughing and he made no further move against Flaubert. I sighed as the boat quietly continued northward. That had been a near one.

Only then, when Weiner sat subdued on his thwart and trailed his hand in the sea alongside, did I notice Flaubert. He was sitting where Moll had lain previously, on the floor-boards over the bilge between Cambreau and myself. There was no more pain in his face. He was not crying either. Just sitting there, his eyes closing sleepily, making no mention of his deplorable existence and his grim persecution.

I glanced at Cambreau, but he did not look at me. He stared straight ahead at the sea, his hair fluttering in the wind.

That was the way the morning passed. . . .

The afternoon prostrated me. The heat was intense. It must have topped one hundred and thirty degrees. It drained out life and left us torpid flesh and sweat. Thinking was impossible in heat like that. Sea and sky were furnace-like. The wind had died and we drifted slowly with the swell, too tired to use the oars. Verne tried to yell us into action, but it was no good. He gave it up shortly. It took too much strength, and he saw that rowing was impossible. We doused ourselves with water, and then had to keep wet. We couldn't let the water dry on us. The burn would have killed us.

Once Pennington said naively: 'It's much warmer, isn't it?'

No one answered.

Only Cambreau stood apart. He did not wet himself. He did not shield himself from the sun. He did not sweat perceptibly.

14

Telez and Verne fought that afternoon and nearly drowned us all.

It was later, much later, when the sun was beginning to wane. The rays did not sting so much any more, but thick, tangible heat still surrounded us. Heat has a real taste after a while. It is creamy and sour, and it coats mouth and gums with a peculiar white fuzz.

DuFond was the cause of the quarrel.

It started in the middle of the afternoon. He grew restless, looking at each of us pleadingly and moving his tongue noisily in his mouth. Every now and then he wiped his lips with the back of his hand and tugged at the neck of his shirt, muttering: 'I'm thirsty.'

Weiner and Telez stared at him when he spoke. But the rest of us pretended we did not hear him.

'I'm thirsty,' he repeated.

We were all thirsty. And every time he mentioned it we squirmed for want of water. We were arid, parched, withered. The sun had done that to each of us, not to DuFond alone. But DuFond had hopes of Verne, felt that Verne might make an exception in his case.

'I'm thirsty,' he said.

'In God's name,' I said, 'do you have to keep saying that?'

'I'm thirsty; I can't help it if I'm thirsty.'

Verne growled: 'Leave him alone, LaSalle!'

'LaSalle is right,' Benet said.

'He'll shut his damn mouth just the same,' Verne said.

I said: 'Not if he keeps squealing.'

Verne didn't know what to do. He couldn't reach me

from the stern. He felt that we were all against him, and he was tired.

DuFond made a face which looked as though he would cry. 'I'm so thirsty. I want a drink of water.'

'Shut up!'

'Just one drink of water. There's the whole keg.' DuFond begged like a child. *I'm so thirsty!*

'All right,' Weiner said. 'I'm thirsty too. Let's all have a drink of water.' He grinned.

Telez said nothing; Flaubert was asleep; I didn't look at Cambreau.

Verne said angrily; 'Cut that out, you!' to Weiner.

'Please, George,' DuFond said, leaning back and stroking Verne's arm. 'Just one swallow. I can't stand this. I'm not like the others. . . . '

Weiner laughed. 'That's the truth, by God!'

'Please, George. . . .'

'I don't think that is fair at all,' Pennington said. 'As for myself, I can do without it. I'm a trifle uncomfortable, but I can do without it. I'm speaking for these others, and I think it's being very unfair.' He wasn't angry. Pennington never got angry. It was as though he were reproving a student.

'I don't care about that,' DuFond said, narrowing his eyes. 'I want a drink. I don't want to burn up. I want a drink!'

I saw Telez lick his lips hungrily.

'George, George,' DuFond went on pleadingly, 'just one swallow, please, just one swallow?' He continued to stroke Verne's arm, wrist to elbow and back again, slowly.

Verne fought against the plea. He tried to evade DuFond. He wanted DuFond's attention, but he foresaw mutiny. There was indecision in his eyes.

'Please, George. . . . '

Telez sighed. His lips were puffed and roughened. He was thirsty too. His patience had broken. He wanted a drink badly. Which one of us didn't? He knew he couldn't have it, and DuFond made thirst so much more real. So when DuFond parted his lips to beg again, Telez turned slowly and rapped him solidly across the mouth with his toughened, opened hand.

'God-damn!' Weiner said, breathing excitedly. 'And a good thing too! He had it coming. Good work there, little Jesus!'

DuFond recoiled violently after the blow, and started to wail. 'George! George!'

Verne, furious, dropped the tiller. He leaned forward and pounded his big fists into Telez's kidneys – hard jarring blows. Telez's face wrinkled and his body jerked with each dull impact. He tried to turn around and face Verne to defend himself, but he couldn't. Verne was hitting him too quickly and too hard, and DuFond had grabbed the shoulder of his shirt and was shaking him to and fro, crying spitefully: 'Hit him, hit him!'

The sloop rocked. It brought the lifeless boom swinging over sharply and it struck DuFond solidly in the back, making him grunt. He released Telez's shirt and clawed at the boom, pushing it away from him in shocked surprise.

Telez made good use of that moment. He raised his right fist and swung it straight down at DuFond's face. It caught him on the bridge of the nose, slid down, lacerated his lower lip and then careened off. It was a good blow. DuFond slipped down off the cross-beam on to the floorboards, where he reposed limply, his nose bleeding.

Verne stopped his blows for a second to see how seriously DuFond was hurt. Telez turned, and I saw the sun glisten by his hand. His knife was out.

Verne paled. Steel was a different matter. He fell back into his stern seat and stared up at Telez, who had risen to his feet, the knife held over his head.

'No,' Telez said suddenly. 'Why stain it?' And he hurled the weapon overboard with a savage gesture.

Verne watched it sink from sight. He was very white. It

60

made his beard look so much the redder. He watched Telez sit down quietly. He didn't say anything.

'You're all right, little Jesus,' Weiner said loudly. 'By God, you're all right with me!'

'Shut up,' Verne said.

'Go to hell,' Weiner said. 'I'm not afraid of you.' He sounded as though he meant it. It did him good to find that Verne was a coward too.

Verne was trying to catch his breath. That knife had taken something out of him. He knew that Telez could have killed him where he sat. Now that the blade was gone he might have gone ahead and pummelled Telez again.

But he didn't. Telez had awed him.

He tried to take it out another way. He thought he could punish us all for siding with the Spaniard. 'Swine,' he said, spitting. 'DuFond drinks all he wants to, you hear that? He can have his drink.'

'If he drinks,' I said, 'then we all do.'

'He drinks all he wants,' Verne said. 'And you swine don't get a drop, not a drop!'

'You try to do that,' Weiner said ominously, 'and we'll throw you overboard.'

Verne pretended he hadn't heard Weiner. He sat back at the stern, holding the tiller again. With his free hand, he leaned over the side and scooped handfuls of sea water on to DuFond's bloody face. He asked anxiously: 'Jacques, Jacques – are you all right?'

DuFond was not all right. He was unconscious. He remained that way until evening when the clouds in the northeast came down on us and a blinding windless rainstorm fell, cooling our burnt skins and refreshing us.

15

After the rain, the wind sprang up. It was a strong twenty-knot breeze, unlike the other, and when it filled the sails it heeled the sloop over at an angle. It came from the south and gave us a stride that was breathtaking. Astern we left a boiling wake of phosphorescence in the darkness. At the bow the white comb rose higher and wider, and now had a high singing voice. That heeling and the sudden charge of the sloop made me feel strong. There was a kind of power in this plunging across the sea. Verne had his hands full with the tiller. He had to keep weathering his helm to hold the boat's head off the wind. The others were quiet, balancing themselves against the angle. A running swell, long and deep, came on from the south. It ran faster than we did. The result was that we kept pitching nose down, sending up cascading geysers of spray which soaked us all to the skin. There was nothing to bail with. Some one began to shovel the water out with cupped hands. I couldn't see who it was. It was too dark to see any of them, except Cambreau.

Next to me, very close, his face looked white in the night. He held it high, nostrils quivering, eyes wide as the seas increased with each forward plunge.

Once DuFond asked timidly: 'Is it all right? Are we safe? The boat is tipping. . . .'

No one answered him. All of us were too much occupied with the pitching and rolling.

I was tired, but I could not sleep. It was thrilling, riding with the wind like that. It was the first time I had ever done it. I liked the sting of the salt spray against my cheek. Sometimes it was needle-like, sometimes very soft. There were tears in my eyes from the bite.

After a while Cambreau glanced at me and asked: 'How do you like it?'

'It's breath-taking,' I said. 'I've never been in a blow before.'

'A blow?' he said, laughing. 'You make it sound big.'

'It is big,' I said. 'Look at those waves.'

'They're not large,' he said.

'They seem so to me,' I said. 'Look at them. I don't know what you'd call a blow. It takes something to make them that high.'

'This is a good wind,' he said. 'That's all.'

'Yes?' I said. 'And what would you call yesterday's?'

'A zephyr,' he said.

'Two points rougher,' I said, 'and we'd have a gale.'

That seemed to amuse him. He laughed pleasantly and turned to the bow again as we pitched erratically, running fast.

'Wait,' he said. 'You'll see a gale soon. Day after tomorrow you'll see a real gale. It will sweep us clear to Trinidad. You'll see some waves, then, running twenty and thirty feet high.'

'Really?' I said.

'They're beautiful!' he said. 'Wait till you see them. It will be a hard gale, out of the southwest. The ceiling will come down on us, grey clouds, and the horizon will close in like a dungeon. In the trough you won't be able to see anything but mountains of green water fore and aft. Then we'll rise as the next crest picks us up, and for a second we'll be able to see the crest coming after that, maybe two hundred feet away. But before you can measure it, in the rolling motion, it will hit us and we'll go speeding down into the trough again. . . . White-caps? Foam, Doctor, foam! It boils all around! When a crest strikes your stern too soon, perhaps after a pause in the trough, boiling foam will rush along your beam level with the gunwale, spitting, hissing, until you'll feel as though you're sitting in the sea itself! Then sometimes the wind catches the spray on top of a crest and then you can see the foam fantail along the ridge like dust from a furrow!'

'I don't know,' I said. 'You make it sound exciting, the way you say it, but it's dangerous. This is a small boat.'

'Are you afraid?' he asked.

'Yes,' I said. 'This boat is too frail for a storm like that.'

'Don't worry,' he said. 'The sloop will survive everything it meets.'

'I wish I could believe you,' I said.

'Doctor,' Cambreau said, 'I have told you that we will meet a gale day after tomorrow. You believe that so much that it worries you. Then I tell you that you will be unharmed by the gale. Why don't you believe that? How can you believe me once and not twice?'

'I don't know,' I said.

'You mustn't be afraid. Never be afraid of anything.'

'That's foolish advice,' I said.

I thought I had hurt him. He didn't reply at once. He was quiet for a few seconds before he said: 'A man who has made a god of fear is an unhappy man.'

'That's true enough,' I said. 'But how can I help being afraid? Look at Moll. It's easy for you to say nothing can harm me. But suppose that snake had bitten me in the ankle. I'd be dead now. I'd be floating back there somewhere instead of Moll.'

'No you wouldn't,' he said.

'What do you mean?'

'We must fear in this life solely because we have to overcome fear. When we have succeeded, we have become perfect.' I didn't understand him. He went on: 'Why didn't the snake bite me when I found it that first night?'

'But – you didn't touch it, did you?'

'I did,' he said.

'And it didn't bite you?'

64

'Why should it have bitten me? I was not afraid of it. It was not afraid of me.'

'Are you saying it bit Moll because he was afraid of it?'

'No,' he said. 'With Moll it was different. He wasn't afraid of it, but he was afraid of something else, an illusion which was so real he lived his life in dread of it.'

I asked: 'What was that?'

'Death,' he said.

'Is that why the snake bit him? Was it predestined?' The spray hit me and I wiped it from my face. 'That would be fatalism.'

'If it hadn't been the snake,' Cambreau said, 'it would have been something else. Moll had to meet it.'

'All right,' I said. 'He met it. He's dead. That's a lovely philosophy of life!'

Cambreau sighed. 'When is a man dead? . . .' There was a long silence while we plunged. I braced myself against the side of the hull. I rocked with the motion and waited ages for him to continue. . . .

'Doctor, you're a medico.'

'I was,' I said.

'Oh, that,' he said. 'That was a lovely thing. Your whole life has been filled with lovely things. You aren't bitter about that. You'd do it again.'

'How do you know?' I asked.

'She was so young and frightened. And you were being kind. You knew the dangers, you fought with yourself about the risk. You didn't think of your reputation, the career you had to boast of; your fears were for her, unknown to you before she came to you; and you sacrificed everything for her.'

'Why that, then?' I asked. 'Why did she have to die? And why did I have to kill the child?'

'As for the child,' Cambreau said, 'it was only an idea, unexpressed. You killed nothing. Do you know why she came to you?'

'She said she was afraid.'

65

'Of what?'

'She said she was afraid of her family, of her friends.'

'That wasn't it,' Cambreau said. 'She wasn't afraid of them. They all knew about it. You learned that when you were tried.'

'That's so,' I said.

'She was afraid of death, like Moll,' he said. 'She was afraid she might die delivering the child. That was why she came to you.'

I shook my head sadly. 'Well, she met what she feared. She died. What good did it do her?'

He smiled. 'She was ready for it. She will never have to do it again.'

'Again?' I echoed.

'Yes,' he said. He did not explain further. 'Some day soon you will understand that.'

I reached out in the darkness and touched his wet arm. I felt it, felt his flesh, wet and cold like my own. 'You are real, aren't you?' I asked.

'Real,' he said.

'You're a man?' I said.

'A man,' he said.

'Are you human?'

'No man is human,' he said. 'When you say human you imply that man is something merely mortal. Mortality is a fear. Men hate mortality. That's why it claims them.'

I said emptily: 'I'm trying to understand, but I can't. What can I believe? I've been a doctor. I've seen the quick and the dead. I've seen men die like Moll last night. Is there anything immortal in the rotting flesh of a corpse? Did you ever see one? Once I had to perform an autopsy on a man who had been dead four months. I wish you could have seen him. There was nothing immortal about that body. It was dead, dead and decayed.'

'There is more to a man than the medium you see him in,' Cambreau said. 'Man is the animation of a shell. The trouble with you, Doctor, is that you believe your body is alive. It isn't. Your body is no more alive than the corpse you autopsied. It is *you* who are alive, it is *you* who are animating that lifeless flesh.'

'But who am *I*?'

He smiled and said nothing.

'You say my body is lifeless,' I went on, 'but that *I* am alive. In that case my body can feel no pain, can never know death because it has no life to lose.'

'Believe that,' he said soberly. 'That is the ultimate truth.'

'I want to believe it,' I said; 'but how can I? How can I believe something which my eyes deny, my nose denies, my ears deny? I felt Moll when I buried him. He was cold, dead. I saw him die. I smelled his rotting wounds. He's dead. How can I believe otherwise?'

'If the body has no life,' Cambreau said, 'how can its senses dictate what is life and what is death? It must naturally contradict itself. You cannot see that yet. But when you have understood just once that you are real and your body is flesh, only a medium of reflection, you will be amazed at the incongruity of your present beliefs.'

'But will I understand?' I asked.

'Yes.'

'When?'

'Very soon now. It is not your turn yet.'

'Not my turn? . . .' I said in a whisper. 'You mean that we are all to have our turn – all of us in this sloop?'

He said: 'That is the reason I am here.'

'You aren't a convict,' I said.

'No.'

'Was Moll – first?'

He nodded.

'And who is next?' I asked.

'George Verne,' he said.

I felt very cold. I asked after a moment: 'What is going to happen to him? What are you going to do to him?'

'I?' Cambreau said. He laid his hand on my shoulder

assuringly. 'You're afraid of me again. I told you not to be. I shall do nothing to Verne. I cannot judge another man. He must judge himself.'

There was a pause.

'Verne,' he said slowly, 'has already destroyed himself.' He looked at me and added: 'Don't look so tragic.'

The sloop rose and fell into each trough. The wind continued to push us hard. There were clouds covering the sky, no moon, no stars, no light at all. Just water and wind and the fleeing boat. . . . It was late when I fell asleep and this night I did not dream at all.

16

Pennington continued to amaze me. He was up with the dawn, energetic, happy, looking marvellously well. The pinched pallid aspect of tuberculosis had disappeared. He glowed. He did not cough any more. But I had seen his symptoms in the past and I could not believe that he would not die. At the colony he had been too far gone. Indeed, the very fact that he suddenly blossomed led me to believe the end was not far off. It's like that with tuberculosis. You feel fine one day and then you suddenly die.

When I awakened next morning he was talking with Cambreau. He said: 'I confess I am at loss to understand this phenomenon. Heretofore I existed, nothing more. I was always sickly, from the time I was a child. There was a period when I liked the idea very much. It was something I could count on – death and a grave. There are so few things a man can count on. But after a while I changed. Not in health. I have always been ill, as I said. But the idea of death lost its lure.'

'Why?' Cambreau asked.

'Well, you see, death then had been so final to me. I was born and raised in Dadeville, Alabama, and my father was a Baptist minister who believed heartily in the vengeance of the Lord and the terrible day of resurrection. He used to berate me daily with pictures of the fiery hell which awaited me if I did not behave. He was righteous, too righteous.'

'Self-righteous, perhaps,' said Cambreau.

Pennington smiled.

'Exactly. Well, he made himself too vehement on the

after life. Instinctively I doubted him, and believed instead that death was finality; I wanted no hell, no judgement, no resurrection, I counted on death as the end. No more afterward. The sweet eternal rest and that sort of abracadabra.'

'Well,' Cambreau said amusedly, 'isn't it that?'

'What?'

'The sweet eternal rest?'

'I think not, now,' Pennington said smiling. 'It's something more.'

'LaSalle doesn't think so,' Cambreau said.

'I'm not afraid of it – judgement and all that,' I said. 'That isn't it. It's just – well, just that I think it finality.'

'You think of it that way because of all the man-made superstition and grief which goes with it.' Pennington spoke absently. 'You've built up a mirage about death, making it omnivorous, Omega. You say to yourself, death is unpleasant, death is real. Ultimately, if not now, I am going to die. How final! How inexorable! Then, because it's the least unpleasant thought, how permanent. And a grave is such a quiet place.'

Pennington sighed sadly. 'At least,' he continued, 'that is what *I* thought, except that I really liked the idea. One lived one's life. One died. That was that. I wanted the quietude of that grave. . . . How foolish I was!'

'I know the feeling,' I said. 'I had it often in the colony. Why is it foolish?'

'Because it is an incongruity,' said Pennington. 'A grave. . . . What is a grave? Tell us, Cambreau.'

'A grave,' he said, 'is a cavity in the earth, dug to receive itself.'

'That's it!' Pennington said. 'How neatly you put it! What has changed when a man dies? Where has the man gone? The body is the same. Why isn't it still a man?'

'Because it is dead,' I said.

'The body?'

'Yes.'

70

'But was it alive before? Was it the body that was alive or was it the man in the body?'

'You mix me up,' I said. 'I can't keep up with you. And – it's odd – you talk like him, like Cambreau.'

'But,' Pennington went on, 'you *know* that there is something more to you than your flesh. Yet you can't seem to admit it. You're afraid to admit it. You've lived your life believing in your flesh. You were a doctor, weren't you? Could you ever touch the power behind the flesh, the vital force which quickened the flesh and marked it a man instead of a corpse? . . . No. That is why I lost my belief in death's finality.'

'All right,' I said. 'Let's consider it. You – the *you* which is real, according to your own concept – is unearthly. It comes from nowhere and quickens your body for a while, then departs into nowhere again. How can a man believe in something he cannot see with his own eyes? What is this thing the spirit? Where does it come from and where does it go? Where is it born and where does it die?'

'It is never born,' Cambreau said. 'It *is*. It never had a beginning and it will never have an end.'

'Then what dies?' I said, straining. 'Tell me what dies! Moll was with us two days ago. Where is he now? Is he alive again?'

'Still.'

'But how? Not that same body.'

'No.'

'That body is dead then?'

'That body is inactive. It cannot die. It was not alive in the first place. I have said this before.'

I stared at him.

'Then where is Moll? Alive, you say? In another world? Tell me.'

'No,' he said. 'These things you must find out for yourself.'

17

There was no sun that day, nor sky either. The grey clouds lay like a low ceiling right over our heads, layer on layer, the colour of soot-covered snowbanks. They hemmed us in ominously, seeming almost close enough to touch. The wind had strengthened, the ridges of the swells were farther and farther apart, and the glassy valleys between them were deepening all the time. There were no more wrinkles on the crests; only the churning foam, studded with white boils which the wind whipped into the air.

We had our rations, hardtack and two swallows of water. When I held the keg it felt much lighter. Eight men had sapped it. There was only a little water left.

It was just as well the sun stayed away.

Verne didn't eat. He took his share of water but refused the hardtack. It made my skin prickly. All I could think was: here's a condemned man. He's got a feeling that he's next, that he's going to die; that's why he can't eat. I wonder if he can actually feel that he's going. And I wonder how he's going to do it.

I was over-sentimental. Verne's real reason for refusing food became evident shortly. He wasn't hungry because there was something on his mind.

DuFond.

He watched the boy, hawk-like, his eyes narrowed, his face screwed up tight. He wanted DuFond so badly he couldn't think of anything else.

18

'I don't like this,' I said to Cambreau when the threatening darkness encompassed us. The sky had lowered until I felt that it was smothering us. The horizon was gone. There was no fog – that wasn't it. But out where the horizon should have been a wall of dense clouds had come down and sealed us tightly into an olive-coloured room. The angry sea was rising, threatening to push us up against the ceiling of the storm and crush us. I had to grip the thwart tightly with both my hands – the motion of the sloop was jerky and violent. It was not the pitching which threw us about. You could get used to that. It was the rolling, long wild sloops from side to side. The mast rocked far over and then far back, over and over again, shuddering with the force of each roll until I wondered how it stayed in its step or why it did not snap off at the top or why we didn't capsize completely. . . . Once I nearly lost my balance, and went cold as ice inside. My mouth kept watering – I had to swallow constantly. I was soaking wet, of course; we all were. I remember thinking: the boat doesn't have to sink, we'll be drowned without turning over. Spray was hitting us hard, slashing into our faces. But we shipped surprisingly little water. I couldn't understand that at all; each comber thundered up behind us, lifted us on its back, the foam racing right at the edge of our gunwale, no more than a precious inch between us and the sea. And then, after the rise, the crest would swish past and the bow sink safely into the smooth, glistening trough. The puny bowsprit of the sloop stabbed into the ocean like a sword, lunging far down, burying its point deep into the sea, then lifting slowly out again. The sails would flap for a second, as if becalmed. Then the next rolling crest would shoot underneath us breaking over the stern where Verne sat fighting the tiller as it swung savagely, trying to shove him away and overboard. Up in the rigging the wind hummed darkly, the only voice audible above the hissing foam and breaking crests.

The storm taxed every muscle. It wouldn't let us relax. We sat there, clinging, waiting for some slight respite, and none came at all. The sway continued to hurtle us back and forth until we were almost ready to let go and drown. Almost. . . .

I gripped my thwart and watched the waves. They were steely-grey where there was no foam, but now and then when they pounded and ran high alongside I could see bilious green, and sometimes dark blue bursts of flashing light for brief seconds. It was terrifying.

The sloop fought to keep its speed in the deep valley of the crests, with the awesome ridge of the next comber rolling down at its stern. It was a nasty thing to see – those hungry mountains of ocean fore and aft, seething with fury as they came, clutching out greedily.

I clawed at Cambreau's shoulder once, and gasped: 'I'm afraid! I don't like this!'

My voice was whipped away in the roar of the wind and the thunder of the waves. 'What did you say,' he yelled his words and then cupped his hand over his ear.

'We're foundering!' I said. 'We're –' I didn't finish. A thin slice of sea struck me across the face and nearly choked me. I swallowed salt water.

Flaubert's shrill voice came to me over the tumult. 'Save me! Save me! We're going to drown! Poor Rudolph is going to drown!' I saw him beating his chest frenziedly before a sheet of jagged spray cut him off from sight. 'God hates me! He's going to drown me with all the rest!' He cried it in a sharp monotone which came through the wind and water with weird clarity. It made me shudder, the tremor racking me so much I nearly released my

74

thwart. For the moment I forgot everything but Flaubert's distorted face, his mouth spread wide, his tongue protruding.

Weiner called forward angrily and when I could see again he was punching Flaubert in the back. He didn't hit him hard, just startled him, and said: 'Cut out that crying, you crazy bug! If I've got to drown I want to do it without your God-damn mercy-on-me chorus!'

'You're trying to kill me!' Flaubert screamed.

I said: 'Leave him alone,' to Weiner.

'God Almighty,' Weiner shouted, 'I'm not hurting him! I want him to lay off that God-damn crying; he's getting on my nerves, he'll have me as crazy as he is! Cut it out, you idiot, cut it out! Nobody's trying to kill you. Shut up!'

'Aoow!' Flaubert wailed, sinking down into the bilge and covering his head with his hands. 'We're going to die!'

I saw Louis Benet then. He had wrapped his arms and legs around his thwart and was clinging frantically as he jerked with the jolting roll. His eyes – dead white against the olive hue of his skin – bulged from their sockets, following a line along the gunwale as each crest ran swiftly by the port quarter. His face was so close to the surface of the crests as they passed that the bursting air bubbles made him blink his eyes. He never said a word.

Pennington called to Cambreau. 'Are we going to get through this?'

'Of course we are!' Cambreau said.

'All of us?'

'Not all of us.'

'Will I?'

Cambreau laughed. 'Are you afraid, professor?'

'I wanted to know, that's all.'

'You'll make it,' Cambreau said.

'It's quite a spectacle,' Pennington said. 'I've never seen the ocean like this before.'

Far astern Telez sat watching Cambreau. I could see his

lips move. *'Es un diablo, ese hombre.'* DuFond was at his left, a pale white face in the half-gloom, taut as a violin string. I couldn't see Verne at all.

Weiner yelled: 'My God, don't this ever stop? I'm getting sick!'

Louis Benet looked around frantically. 'Not in here, please, not in here,' he said. 'I couldn't stand that. Not in here. Over the side.' I remember that impressed me deeply at the time – the fact that a brute capable of raping a little girl could really be bothered by seasickness.

'You go to hell,' Weiner replied weakly. 'I'll get sick where I God-damn please. Leave me alone!'

The mast was creaking like the bones of an old man. The canvas slapped in staccato bursts like gunfire. Up by the jib a stray piece of canvas was dancing crazily. The boom had swung out to port, giving more mainsail area to the gale, and with the increase the sloop lurched dangerously.

I said: *'Verne!'*

No answer. I peered, could see his big bulk by the tiller. He was watching DuFond.

'Verne!'

Benet asked fearfully : 'Doctor – what's the matter?'

I said: 'It's the mast – it won't stand the strain – listen to it! The mainsail will go in a second.' I cupped my hands. 'Verne, for God's sake!'

Verne finally said: 'Mind your tongue! You'll be all right.'

'It's the mast!' I said. 'We've got to shorten sail.'

'It stays there. Mind your tongue, damn you!'

'We're capsizing, you fool. We're capsizing! The mast is going to go, and the sails. Listen to it!'

Verne didn't answer. He kept looking at DuFond.

I called: 'Weiner!'

'What the hell do you want now?'

'Lower the mainsail! We'll capsize if you don't. Haul it down! Pennington – help him.'

'I'm sick,' Weiner said.

'Never mind that! Pennington?'

'All right,' Pennington said.

Together they grasped the halyard and loosened it from the cleat. Then they slacked it off; but the rings on the sail stuck against the mast. Telez stood up and climbed the mast to them while we hauled in the main sheet. When he reached them he wrapped one leg around the mast and threw his weight against the sail, endeavouring to drag it down. The sail began to fall. The sloop stopped lurching as the canvas shortened, but still leaned slightly.

'It's down,' Weiner said. 'And a God-damn good job too! My hands are skinned raw.'

'Furl it. Lash the boom!'

'I'm doing it,' Pennington said.

'Oh, God,' Weiner groaned. 'I'm going to be sick!'

'Not in here,' Benet said.

'Oh, God, I feel awful!' Weiner held his mouth with one hand, a thwart with the other. Pennington called to me: 'He's seasick, Doctor.'

'We can't do anything about that,' I said.

Simultaneously the sound of a faint explosion came from somewhere in the stern, and DuFond's young high voice rang out in a strident scream so filled with terror that even Weiner – who was vomiting over the gunwale with lusty enthusiasm – stopped his retching and glanced aft to see what had happened.

Louis Benet leaned forward and tugged at my leg. He said: 'It was DuFond – DuFond!'

I stood up, my legs locked around the thwart on which I had been sitting, and peered astern; but I couldn't see a thing. It was raining now, in sudden gusts, the drops hitting us like bullets and bringing with them a thick gloomy mist. I yelled: 'Telez! Jesus Telez!' to the Spaniard.

'*Si! Si!*' His voice was taut and far away, and it floated forward to me fantastically from the sheets of rain which hid him from my sight.

'What happened?'

'*El perro peludo!*'

DuFond screamed again, this time intelligibly: 'He's gone! He's gone!'

'Verne's overboard!' Weiner yelled at me. 'God-damn it – Verne's overboard!'

There was nothing to do. Verne was gone. No man could have lived in that sea. We couldn't go back. We couldn't even attempt to best that gale with oars. They'd have snapped in the rowlocks. We could never have found him. I couldn't even see Jesus Telez in the stern. How could we have found Verne then, hidden not only by the wall of the rain but also by the mountains of ocean? . . .

Telez passed the word along through Weiner. He couldn't yell loudly enough to be heard at the bow. Weiner leaned over and told me what had happened.

It was the mainsail. Verne had been tugging with one hand at the leech of the mainsail to help bring it down, and steering with the other while he watched DuFond and cursed the storm.

But a sudden gust filled the sail and the flailing canvas enveloped Verne as it fell. Verne, terrified by this, tore at it with both his hands, releasing the tiller as he did so. Then everything seemed to go against him.

The sail covered him. A wave hit the stern, swung the tiller hard against his side, the stern leaped up and Verne – his body travelling with the impetus of the blow from the tiller – catapulted over the side and into the water. Telez said he did not even see him land. The night and the ocean and the wind and the rain ate him alive.

Through all this Cambreau sat at the bow facing forward, his eyes fixed on the giant crests which came up under the bowsprit and rolled on and away; his hair blowing freely despite its wetness; his face shining somehow as the spray whipped over it.

The gloom of the storm had faded now into the blackest night I ever saw, black and thick and tangible, loud with the sound of wind and rain and roaring sea.

None of us slept.

19

The next day was just as bad. No sun, no daylight, only a blanket of murk, pierced by jagged bolts of lightning while the splitting bass of the thunder made us vibrate right down to our heels. No more riding the thwarts. Too high. You couldn't hang on. We all climbed down and lay on the floor-boards, soaked with the filthy bilge water which slopped to and fro with the muscle-rending roll of the sloop. Weiner became terribly sick. So did Telez. Pennington, his face close to mine, said: 'I have just realized how insignificant a man can be. . . .' Louis Benet's eyes rolled. His skin was dark green now; fear had drained the blood from it. Flaubert did not wail any more. He couldn't open his mouth. The bilge water stopped that. DuFond looked like a drowned rat, his face whiter than the whites of Benet's eyes. Cambreau lay with his eyes closed. I stared at the serenity of his face.

Sometimes there were lightning bolts that we could not see. We could just catch their flare, quick ruddy blossomings of brilliant light, and the thunder far away, muttering as it came down. The seas were enormous and the wind a nightmarish blast which shook the fighting sloop with awful shudders from stem to stern.

We had kept the jib up in order to give the boat her head, but not for long. A dull boom told us when it blew out, and when it went, it went so thoroughly that not a shred remained. It was ripped away bodily, every inch of its canvas, and where it disappeared to we never knew, because when we looked up, all we could see was the empty triangle of rope which had contained it although the echo of its explosive departure still rang in our ears.

I knew what a gale was now. It was a world of hostile ocean gone suddenly and violently mad.

I prayed that night for the first time in twelve years.

20

Next morning, I found that the ocean could be a hypocrite. The mountains of water had vanished. There were only the choppy waves and erratic swells, not steep at all, and no white-caps. After a few hours of cloudiness, the sun broke through the mist and made the ocean look still more harmless. Compared to the night before, everything seemed peaceful and gentle. You could almost see the ocean gloating with satisfaction, smacking its lips with the taste of Verne. I shivered. I wasn't glad that Verne was dead. That was an awful way to go.

We had lost our food and water, as we discovered when DuFond lifted his furtive eyes and said: 'Can I have my swallows? I'm thirsty.'

'Sure,' I said.

'Where the hell do you get that stuff?' Weiner barked at me importantly. 'I'm in charge now and you'll all God-damn well do what I say, understand?'

'Are you the dictator again?' I asked.

'You heard me,' he said.

'Moll had to die first in order for you to be dictator,' I said. 'Then Verne had to die. Why weren't you dictator when Verne was alive?'

'You shut your mouth!' he said, snapping.

I said: 'I didn't see you doing any dictating when Verne was here.'

'I wasn't afraid of Verne,' he said. 'You heard me tell him where to go. Verne didn't have the guts of a louse. You heard me tell him where to go all right.'

'He couldn't hurt you way back in the stern,' I said.

'I told him. And I'm telling you.' Weiner pulled down

his lips and tried to look tough.

I laughed harshly. 'All right. You're the dictator. Hail Weiner!'

'Cut that out!' he said balefully.

'You weren't doing much dictating last night,' I said. 'I guess dictators aren't at their best when they're vomiting. Is that right? . . . Can't a dictator dictate when he's seasick?'

'You God-damn quack,' Weiner said. 'When we get ashore, I'll beat your brains in!'

I asked evenly: 'Why wait until we get ashore?'

'Shut your trap! Hear me?'

'Go on,' I said wearily. 'Dictate the boy into a drink of water.'

'He'll drink when I say so.' Weiner said.

'Then don't say so,' Pennington said in a low voice. 'The keg is gone; so is the food.'

They'd been swept overboard some time during the night. I remember seeing them before darkness. They must have been pitched out or washed overboard. Anyway, they were gone. None of us would get a drink of water.

This crushed DuFond. He pulled at his throat and quietly retreated to his thwart in the stern. He was afraid now, more than before. A ring of hostility surrounded him. He could feel it. No Verne, no protection. He was on his own and he didn't like it. He was afraid.

Telez held the tiller. A brisk wind filled the canvas and pushed us on. We didn't know where we were at all. The compass had been smashed to pieces. We steered by the sun, heading west with the wind abeam which filled our only sail – the mainsail – with its breath.

Weiner was flabbergasted. He was as hungry and as thirsty as the rest of us and he didn't like being dictator of a crew that lacked food and water. Regarding us all warily he said: 'All right now, men, we'll get along. Don't worry about the water. We'll be reaching land soon now and we'll get some more.'

'You don't believe that,' Cambreau said.

I looked at him. He had turned around from his seat in the bow and watched Weiner with quiet eyes. In the stern, Telez's lips moved soundlessly and I saw him cross himself.

Weiner tried to avoid Cambreau's eyes. 'Don't tell me what I believe. We'll get water. You heard me.'

'You don't believe it,' said Cambreau. 'You're saying that because you're afraid we won't.'

'I'm not!'

'Yes, you are,' Cambreau said.

'I'm not, God-damn it, I'm not!'

Cambreau sighed. 'Poor Weiner,' he said softly. 'Blustering to bluff his own fear. Blustering to bluff the men around him. Blustering and blustering because it hurts to be a failure.'

Weiner stared at him.

'Yes,' Cambreau said, 'it hurts to be a failure. When you know yourself that you are a failure, it hurts. So bluster, and make your comrades afraid of you, and then they'll think you the man of strength which you know you are not.'

Weiner looked very pallid.

'Don't worry,' Cambreau said finally. 'We'll get water.'

'Will we? Will we?' DuFond asked before he realized he had spoken and when he heard his own voice, he covered his mouth and cringed back, afraid of rebuke.

'How can you tell?' Weiner asked suddenly.

'We'll have water very shortly,' Cambreau said. 'We are going to reach Trinidad to-day. You'll see the island soon.'

'Trinidad!' Weiner exclaimed.

'Is that French?' Benet asked anxiously.

I said: 'It's British.'

'We can't stop there,' Benet said. 'They'll capture us and send us back! It's the same as their Guiana! They send you back from there.'

'They won't send you back,' Cambreau said.

Weiner asked warily: 'Who are you anyway? How can you know all this?'

'That man is a devil,' Telez said from the stern. 'He knows everything. He knows things he has not seen or heard. He made Moll die and he made Verne die. He is a devil.'

He spoke in Spanish which nobody understood but Pennington and myself.

Pennington said to Telez: *'No, no, es un angel.'*

'Un diablo. Lo sé. Es un diablo!'

Pennington looked at me. 'How can a man be so blind?'

Telez crossed himself when Cambreau laughed.

'Pardon me,' Benet said presently, cocking his greasy face humbly to one side and lifting his left shoulder slightly, 'but you are sure about Trinidad? The British are likely to return convicts.'

'I'm certain,' Cambreau said. 'They won't send *us* back.'

'You see,' Benet said, rubbing his hands gingerly, 'I once knew an ace at the colony who made an escape and reached the free soil of Venezuela. And right there, with freedom in his grasp, he ran into some British blacks from the Guiana and they captured him and sent him back. The British are very exacting when it comes to extradition. But if you're sure –'

'I'm sure,' Cambreau repeated.

'Well, then I suppose it's all right,' Benet agreed smoothly. 'Of course you understand that I am not attempting to make myself unnecessarily the complainer of this party, nor do I intend to make you think that I am trying to dictate to any one, but the thought of Trinidad disturbed me a trifle. We've come so far, you see, and I would hate to be taken and be returned at this point when I have just reached the chance where I can begin my new life again. That was always my dream, you know, to begin again and wipe out the memories of the strange condition which brought me into the colony. All these years, I waited and saved and now that life is opening its doors to me again and I have the golden opportunity to start it anew without the handicap of my past, I am very anxious to do so and to prove that I can be as good and upright a citizen as any other man despite –'

'For God's sake!' Weiner said, amazed. 'What the hell's got into Benet? Listen to him chatter! He runs on like an old biddy, by God! He's been vaccinated with a phonograph needle!'

Benet looked pained. 'That's very unkind of you,' he said. 'I was only ascertaining whether or not it was safe for us to put in at Trinidad. I was thinking of you and the others, just as much as I was of myself. The fact that my fears led me to talk too much –'

Weiner laughed and slapped his leg. 'Listen to him. He's a regular cabinet minister. He should make political speeches. By God Almighty, he doesn't even have to take a breath. . . . Go on, Louis, go on, tell us some more about this new and righteous life that you're going to live. We want to hear some more, don't we boys? Louis Benet is going to be upright. He isn't going to rape little girls any more. He's going to rape the big girls now. He's got too big for the little girls so now he's going to rape the big girls and start life all over again with a clean record!'

Benet flushed and his eyes looked guilty. 'That's very unkind –'

'To the little girls?' Weiner said quickly. Then he roared with laughter. 'Oh, my God, this is funny, this is good! Louis is going to be a saint! Saint Louis Benet and his new life!'

'That's very unkind,' Benet repeated.

'St Louis the rapist!' Weiner roared.

'That's very unkind,' Benet said. 'I'm not going to be a saint. But I'm going to lead a new respectable life. I'm a changed man, that's all. You don't know how I've changed.'

Weiner stopped laughing and stared at Benet. 'You don't really believe that, do you?'

'I'm changed,' Benet said, rubbing his hands. 'You can't understand how much I've changed.'

'Listen,' Weiner said evenly, shaking his finger at Benet. 'There's only one way to change a man like you and that's by –'

'Don't say it!' Benet cried. His eyes widened and he shuddered. 'Don't! That's an awful thing to say –'

'It's the God's honest truth,' Weiner said baldly. 'And you know it!'

21

'Land!'

The sloop careened as we all jerked around to see. Telez stood up in the stern, holding the tiller with his knee. It was DuFond who had cried out. He stood erect, pointing his arm dead ahead at the horizon.

'Where?' Weiner asked, peering intently. 'I don't see a God-damn thing but water!'

'It's ahead!' DuFond said. 'Straight ahead! See there!'

'I see, I see,' Flaubert cackled. 'Yes, yes, yes! Land ahead! Oh, how happy I am! Rudolph is saved! Poor Rudolph is happy to be saved!'

'Shut up, you bug,' Weiner said. 'I can't see it yet. Whereabouts?'

'I can't see it,' Benet said. 'I can't see it at all.'

'I can,' said Pennington. 'But it's like smoke.'

'I can see it,' I exclaimed suddenly. 'It's not smoke. It's like a peninsula. It's jutting out there like a finger. It's green, I can see it!'

Cambreau chuckled.

'Can you see it?' I asked.

'Yes, it's Galera Point. I've seen it for the last ten minutes.'

'Galera Point?'

'Yes,' he said. 'The northeast tip of Trinidad. If you look to the north when we pass it, you'll be able to see Tobago. All the Windward Islands run in a string up there. We've got to pass the Galera. We've got to skirt the northern end of the island entirely until we reach a strait known as the Dragon's Mouth. We'll pass through there and you'll see Venezuela on the right when we do.'

'Why so?'

'Well, you see, we've got to reach the Bay of Paria in order to dock in Port of Spain. That's where we're going – to Port of Spain.'

'I know,' I said. 'Then what were you chuckling at?'

He smiled. 'I was chuckling at you.'

'Why?'

'Don't you know yet?' he asked.

'No, or else I wouldn't ask.'

'But it's like you to ask, even when you do know a thing,' he said. 'You're a very inconsistent man. You can remember the oddest things. You can tell me – if I were to ask you – every painful materialization which you saw on Moll as the result of that bite. You always remember pain and disease and imperfection and discord. But when you see perfection and harmony, you cannot recognize it.'

'I have never seen perfection,' I said. 'And as for harmony, I see that in you.'

'Really, then you have noticed that?'

'Yes.'

'And in yourself perhaps?'

'Not in myself,' I said. 'Harmony? Not while I own this body.'

He smiled. 'You mean your hernia.'

'Yes.'

'And your eyesight?'

'Yes.'

'One night within the month,' he said, 'you'll lose that truss and lose it forever.'

'How can that happen?' I asked. 'Do you mean it? Am I going to get this wretched thing patched?'

'Yes.'

'An operation? . . . When and where?'

'At sea,' he said.

'And who is going to operate?' I asked dryly.

'You.'

I felt bitter. 'I thought you meant it. You've been

baiting me. How can I operate on myself? Hernia is a major operation.'

'All operations are the same,' Cambreau said. 'This one will be your own triumph. There'll be no scalpel. There will only be your own thought. And you'll be healed.'

'Healed by thought?' I asked and shook my head. 'That's a beautiful speech, though the project is utterly and humanly impossible.'

'I made no mention of the word humanly,' he said.

'It is impossible!' I said.

Turning to the prow he pulled me close to him and pointed. 'There is Galera Point.'

'I know, I know,' I said. 'I can see it.'

'It is fifteen miles away.'

'What of it?' I asked.

'Doctor,' he said, 'what did you suffer in your eyes?'

'Acute myopia,' I said. 'And I still *do* suffer. Nearsightedness. I had it from childhood. I was as blind as a bat until I got my spectacles.'

He sighed and patted my shoulder. 'This time,' he said, 'I have helped you. You had to be helped. Next time, you will have to help yourself.'

I frowned.

'What are you talking about?' I asked curiously.

'A man cannot be very nearsighted,' he said, 'when he can make out a point of land against a stretch of sea all of fifteen miles away.'

'Don't be foolish,' I said, 'with my glasses, I can see –' I raised my hand to my face to adjust them and I stopped speaking instantly.

My glasses weren't there.

'Yesterday afternoon,' he said, 'they were pulled off your face in the storm. You didn't know it.'

I took my hand down from my face slowly.

'You can see,' he asked. 'Can't you?'

'Yes,' I replied.

'How far can you see *now*?'

90

'Farther,' I said quietly, 'than Galera Point.'

'Why don't you thank me?'

I said: 'You may have done this for me, but I know that you aren't the one to be thanked.'

'This is more than I expected.'

The continent was shaping itself slowly as we blew down on it from the east.

Part II

*Dig not too narrow,
not too deep, that
I may come forth*

Port of Spain. The waterfront was quiet and industrious.
The city was clean. I liked it. Macadam streets, auto-
mobiles, and fresh white buildings. It was very hot. I
could feel the difference the moment we tied up and the
wind dropped. It made you sweat. The place where we
docked was pretty deserted and the pier itself rotten and
small. There was a man standing on the pier when we
pulled in and dropped the sail. I called: 'Do you own this
pier?'

'No,' he said.

'Is it all right if we tie up here?' I asked.

'Sure,' he said. 'It's all right. Everybody uses it.'

'Thanks,' I said.

We furled the sail and then we made the boat fast
against the creaking logs that supported the pier. It was
low tide, and we were far down below the level of the
pier. We left the lines fairly taut for the rise in tide and
then we climbed up a small ladder to the top of the pier.

It was good to feel earth under foot again but I swayed
a little because I was so used to the motion of the sloop. I
was hungry. I wanted something to eat and had my money
ready. We had all got our money ready long before we
landed. When we scattered, I said: 'We'd better be back
at the boat together by to-night.'

'That's right,' Weiner said. 'Back here to-night to talk
things over. But I tell you one thing. I'll be God-damned
if I ever get in that tub again. This place looks all right to
me.'

'What do you mean?' I asked.

'It's none of your business,' he said, 'but if I like this

place enough, I'm staying here. The hell with fighting a sea like yesterday. I've had my bellyful of that stuff. I'm free, understand? We've made it. Dry land. From now on, we're on our own.'

'All right,' I said. 'That's your affair.'

He departed with an energetic step. DuFond followed him without a word, shadowing his heels.

Telez said: 'I'll be back at the boat. I'm not going to stay here.'

'All right,' I said. I looked at Pennington. 'How about you?'

'I don't know what's going to happen to me,' he replied. 'Perhaps I'll be back at the boat. Perhaps not. There's an American ship in the harbour. I saw her as we came in. I'm going to try and get aboard her.'

'You haven't any passport,' I said.

'No matter,' he said. 'I'm going to try. Perhaps they'll take me.'

Cambreau said: 'They won't take you,' and shook his head.

'I'm going to try anyway,' Pennington smiled. 'No harm trying.'

'What about Flaubert?' I asked. 'We can't leave him to run around loose. He's a responsibility.'

'Yes,' Flaubert said. 'I'm all alone! I can't be left all alone! I'll be afraid all alone! Poor Rudolph, nobody cares about you. . . .'

'I'll take care of you,' I said.

'No,' Cambreau said. 'I'll take care of Flaubert. You go along, Flaubert will be all right with me. I promise you.'

Benet didn't say anything. He stood rubbing his hands and his eyes glowed while he waited for us to finish. Finally we agreed to come back to the boat that night and see what could be done.

I walked into the city alone. People stared at me curiously. They made me aware of my wretched appearance. I had seven days' growth on my face and my clothes were in rags. They made me feel embarrassed.

Presently I passed a barber's shop, turned back and entered it. The barber was sitting in one of his chairs, reading a newpaper. He put it down when he heard me, he got up and offered me a seat.

When he saw me, he gasped. 'Gor!'

'I look a mess,' I said. 'I've been at sea for the last week. We had some rough weather.'

'It must have been rough weather,' he said.

'I've got to get some clothes too,' I said. 'Can you tell me where to pick some up cheap? I'm a stranger here.'

'Well,' he said, 'there's a place a few doors up the street. They have right fine clothes for nothing at all.'

'Thank you,' I said.

'Now let me see,' he said. 'What'll you have done?'

'I want a shave,' I said. 'And a shampoo. Get me all cleaned up. I'm a mess.'

'You are that,' he said. 'All right.'

He went to work and shaved me first. My skin felt smooth and soft when he had finished. 'You didn't come in on one of them big ships, did you?' he asked.

'Oh, no, just an open sloop.'

'First time in Port of Spain?'

'Yes.'

'Bend down your head over this basin. . . . That's it. I've got to soap it thick. . . . What'd you say your last port of call was?'

'I didn't say,' I replied. 'Go easy. That hurts.'

'Sorry,' he said. 'Your hair is tangled like a net. A little sloop, eh? You're not one of them fellows that sails around the world in an open boat, are you?'

I said: 'This was far from being a pleasure cruise.'

'Oh,' he said. 'Business, eh?'

'Necessity.'

'Say!' he exclaimed. He stood off and stared at me a second. 'Say, you aren't one of the escaped convicts from the Guiana?'

I stiffened instinctively, then relaxed. 'How did you know?'

'I just guessed from what you said!'

'I mean – how did you know that any convicts had escaped from the colony?'

'Why, from the newspapers,' he said. 'I was reading about it in the newspapers. There was quite a story, names and everything! Ten of you, Gor, I say, it takes pluck to break away from that hell-hole. You've got my best wishes.'

'Thank you,' I said.

'How'd you ever do it?' he asked.

I hesitated. There was no reward for us now. Betrayal wouldn't mean much to him.

'We just broke away,' I said.

'Gor!' he said. 'Ten of you! It must have been pretty nervy of you. Did you all make it?'

'There were eleven of us,' I said. 'We lost three men.'

'Eleven? Now that's queer. The paper said ten. It gave the names. Not eleven.'

'There were eleven.'

'Eleven in a sloop!' He shook his head. 'I'm glad I wasn't with you. How many days?'

'Five,' I replied. 'We struck a gale yesterday. We lost our food and water and one man. Have you ever been in a gale?'

He grinned. 'Not with my rheumatism!'

'It's something to see,' I said. 'You never realize how unimportant you can be until you ride a gale.'

He said: 'Mister, I'll be unimportant right here on dry land. Gor, I don't see how you made it. By rights you should all be drowned dead. . . . There. That's finished. How do you feel?'

I sighed: 'I feel a thousand times better.'

'Well – you look a little more civilized.' He considered me and then grinned again. 'Say, you're not a bad sort. I bet you'd like a bath.'

96

'That's kind of you. I would.'

'I've got a tub in the back room. It's just a tub and a toilet. If you'd like to use it –'

I said: 'That's decent of you. I appreciate it. But I'd like to get some clean clothes too. Suppose I –'

'Now,' he interrupted. 'Don't you bother. You go in and get your bath. I'll run up and get you the clothes. Have you got any money?'

'Oh, yes, but it's in francs.'

'Francs'll do; I'll get you the clothes and pay for them and you can pay me. Let's see . . . what'll you wear?'

'Get me a pair of white ducks,' I said. 'And some sort of cheap jacket. And a shirt. I'll never forget this. You're very kind. I take a 44 waist size and the trouser length should be 28. Thanks a lot.'

'Ah!' he grunted, 'forget it. I'll be right back. You'll find the tub in the back room. There's soap there too. I won't be long. . . .'

When he came back, I was rinsing the soap off myself. He appeared with a white canvas coat, a pair of ducks, a white shirt, and even had a striped tie. He put them on a chair, grinning. 'A royal outfit, mister, and it cost practically nothing. There's a towel right behind you. What's your name?'

'LaSalle,' I said. 'What's yours?'

'Berry,' he said. 'John Berry.'

'Are you English?'

'Me English? Hell, mister, I'm as much a Yank as George Washington! I was born in Ithaca, New York.'

'I'm an American myself,' I said.

'No!' he said. 'I thought' you were French with a name like you have!'

'No,' I said. I got out of the tub, found the towel, and dried myself.

'Say,' he said, 'how about underwear?'

'I'll get along without that. Thanks just the same.' I tossed the towel aside and picked up the truss and put it on. The leather had an evil smell, but nothing could be done about it. When he handed me my trousers, Berry said: 'Awful thing, that. Bother you much?'

'Yes,' I said.

'I know a man who died from it,' he said.

'Lots of them do,' I said. When I had finished dressing I glanced at myself in the mirror. I looked very good, white, clean, and healthy, though a trifle thin. 'This is fine. You've been more than kind, Mr Berry. I'll not forget it.'

'Gor!' he dismissed it with a wave of his hand.

'How much do I owe you?'

'Let's say a pound.'

I paid him in francs, shook hands with him, and left with his best wishes.

2

I arrived at the pier shortly before dark. The tide had risen and the sloop floated higher so that I could have stepped aboard easily. I didn't step down though. I just gave it a glance, not expecting to find anything. None of the others had returned.

A man was standing on the pier. He had been glancing out on the bay when I appeared, but when he heard the planks creak under my weight, he looked up and regarded me with care. He was young, about twenty-eight, and wore a white linen suit and a Panama hat. He had dark-rimmed glasses which gave him a ludicrously owlish aspect. He seemed half inclined to dismiss my presence altogether until I went over and looked at the sloop. Then he became interested.

I strolled back to the street edge of the pier and stood there absently, wondering when the others would show up and wondering where they could be. . . . After about two minutes I felt the stranger come close to me. Touching his hand to his Panama he said:

'Excuse me . . .'

I turned. 'Yes?'

He continued: 'My name is Meredith. Roy Meredith.'

'Hello,' I said, not too warmly.

'I saw you looking at this sloop,' he said. 'I wondered if you knew anything about it. I'm trying to get in touch with the men who own it.'

'Why?' I asked.

'Well,' he said. 'I'm a newspaper correspondent.'

'What of it?' I asked.

'I'm covering the story,' he said. 'This sloop was used

by ten convicts who escaped from the Guiana. I'd been hoping that they'd reach Port of Spain so that I could get the story. My news service instructed me not to miss it in case it broke here. So I posted a man on the waterfront and kept him in touch with small-boat arrivals and departures. He told me this afternoon that a gang of men arrived in this boat and that they looked as though they might be the convicts. . . . I didn't really believe I'd have the luck to find them putting in here. I thought sure they'd go north to Tobago or south to Venezuela.'

'You sound like an American,' I said.

'I am,' he said, 'I'm a press correspondent. I flew down here from Havana when the revolution quieted down. I just did it on a chance. It's a hell of a good yarn. The men who make a successful break from *that* place you can count on the fingers of your hands. There was a flurry when the story broke last week. . . . I'm with the National News Association in New York.'

'My name is LaSalle,' I said. 'Philip LaSalle. This is the right sloop, Mr Meredith. I came in with her to-day.'

'I thought so!' he exclaimed. 'You look all slicked up now, but the way you looked at the boat, I kind of felt you'd been with her! . . . Will you give me the story?'

'All right, what do you want to know?'

'Have a seat,' he said, 'and wait'll I get this list out.' I sat down on the piling and he sat next to me. He pulled out a piece of paper. 'Let's see. Ten men made the break. That was last Tuesday –'

'Eleven men,' I said.

'That's funny,' he said. 'There are only ten in the list of those escaped. This is the official list.'

'Read it to me.'

'Louis Benet; Jacques DuFond; James Dunning; Rudolph Flaubert; Philip LaSalle; Henry Moll; Richard Pennington; Jesus Telez de la Salinas; George Verne; Carl Weiner.'

'There's one missing,' I said. 'They left out Jean Cambreau.'

'Jean Cambreau?'

'Yes,' I said. 'Cambreau was with us in the escape before Verne came. Verne, you see, forced himself in. He didn't really contribute towards the fund which purchased this sloop. He followed two of the members and when he reached the boat, we let him come.'

'You did? You let him come then?'

'Frankly, Mr Meredith, he assumed charge.'

'I see,' he said. 'And that's how you did it. You paid somebody for a boat. What then?'

'The boat was hidden somewhere. We broke loose from the colony, found the boat and then launched it.'

Meredith shook his head admiringly. 'Can you tell me the name of the man who helped you?'

'No,' I said. 'One day he might do it for some one else. He couldn't if his name were known.'

'I understand,' Meredith said, grinning. 'Confidences of the profession. All I can say is, I think you all had a hell of a lot of nerve. I'd never have made it. Good God, that's all jungle there, isn't it?'

'Yes.'

'And did you all come through?'

'No. Dunning never reached the boat. He died en route, probably from a heart attack. It was a strenuous task, beating that jungle. He wasn't in good shape.'

'Tough,' Meredith said. 'Anyone else?'

'Henry Moll,' I said. 'He died the first night at sea. He was bitten by a fer-de-lance just before he reached the beach.'

'God!' Meredith shuddered.

'Then there was George Verne,' I said. 'He was swept over-board night before last during a gale.'

'Holy Judas! You must have had a tough time! How many of you reached here?'

'Eight of us,' I said.

101

'But you lost three men. Three from ten –'

'Eleven. You forgot Jean Cambreau.'

'But that's damned funny,' he said. 'This is the official list. There's no Cambreau on it. Are you sure he's a convict?'

'No, but he was with us anyhow.'

'What was he in for?'

'I don't know.'

'Who is he? Where's he from?'

'I don't know that either.'

'Well, it's queer,' Meredith frowned. 'I know this is the list. They wouldn't make any mistake about the number of convicts missing.'

I said: 'No, they wouldn't do that.'

'Look here,' he asked then, 'what are your plans for the future?'

'Mine?'

'All of you.'

I shrugged. 'I wish we knew. I'm going on myself. Weiner wants to stay here. He's had enough of the sea. Pennington is trying to get passage on a boat, but I don't think he will. The rest of us will probably sail again. I think I'll head for America. The chances of extradition there are slighter. Change my name and all that. The country's big enough for us to elude the immigration authorities.'

'God,' he said, 'you don't mean anybody would be tough enough to send you *back*?'

'It's been done,' I said. 'Benet was worried about you people here. The British have been very unkind about such things before in the Guiana. However, be a good sport. Better make it – destination unkown.'

'I'll do that,' he said. 'Far be it for me to be in-strumental in pulling you back there. What's it like?'

'Terrible,' I said. 'Any time you're tired of living go down to the sixth parallel. You won't find much to believe in.'

102

'No, thanks.' He shook his head. 'I don't suppose you'd consent to a picture of the whole crew?'

'No,' I said. 'You might snap the boat. But not the crew. It will be hard enough to remain nonentities when we get where each of us is going.'

'That's right. Say, you've been a big help. This will boost my stock no end. Thanks a lot. I'd like to get a look at the others too. Have you any idea where they are?'

'No,' I said. 'But you come around tomorrow and you'll meet them then.'

'All right,' he said. He walked across the pier and stared at the sloop. She was bobbing up and down, the mast swaying with the motion of the tide. 'That's not much of a boat. I don't see how you made it. You said you ran into a storm too. . . . Well, I'm damned if I know how you got here at all. And you're going to sail again in the same tub?'

'We've no other,' I said.

'God!' he said. 'That's taking a chance of losing the whole works. Suppose the thing sank on this next trip after you've made good your escape?'

'There's nothing else to do,' I replied. 'That's all we have.'

'Tell you what,' he said, 'there's a gang of Americans in town. They work here. They're pretty good eggs and they've been reading about the escape and talking about the nerve it took. I'll see what they can do.'

'That's kind of you,' I said. 'Thanks.'

'I'll cable my office to-night too. They may have a brilliant suggestion or two.'

'Thanks.'

'Okeh,' he said. 'I'll call it a night then. Orchids to you for this yarn, LaSalle. I'll see you in the morning.'

'All right,' I said. 'I'll be seeing you.'

3

It got dark and the stars came out and the city bloomed with electricity. I sat on the pier for a long time, watching the tide come in until I could see the top of the sloop's gunwale from right where I was. I kept waiting, but none of the others came back at all and I began to get worried.

After a long while, a man came down the waterfront street. He stopped in front of the pier and glanced down at the sloop. He nodded to himself, satisfied, and then walked out on the pier and saw me sitting on the piling. He wore the uniform of the Trinidad police. He had a pleasant face, and nice eyes. He nodded to me and said: 'Good evening.'

'Hello,' I replied.

'This is the convict boat, isn't it?' he asked.

'I wouldn't know,' I said warily.

'I'm looking for a Dr LaSalle,' he said. 'Dr Philip LaSalle.'

'I never heard of him,' I said.

'Now,' he said, 'you don't have to lie. You must have heard of him. You're one of the convicts, aren't you?'

'What makes you think so?' I asked.

'One of your men told me that you were all supposed to meet back here at the boat tonight. Why else are you here?'

'Who told you that?' I asked.

'A man named Louis Benet,' he said.

'Where is he?' I asked.

'At police headquarters,' he said. 'I want a man named Dr LaSalle.'

'What for?'

'If you're afraid that you'll be held for extradition,' he replied, 'I'll tell you frankly that that isn't the case at all.'

'Then what is the case?' I asked.

'That will be explained by the magistrate,' he said. 'Are you Dr LaSalle?'

'I have never heard of him,' I said. 'I never heard of Louis Benet either.'

'There's no use lying,' he said cheerfully. 'I think you're suspicious so I'll take you in charge anyway.'

'You can't do that.'

'Yes, I can,' he said. 'You may as well own up.'

I got to my feet and sighed. 'All right. I'm LaSalle.'

'Very good,' he said, unsurprised. 'Please walk ahead of me to the police station. Three blocks down the waterfront and then turn to your right.'

We walked down the waterfront and I felt very grateful for the courteous way the arrest was being handled. The policeman was quite polite about the whole thing and he didn't make it embarrassing by walking along beside me or holding my shoulder. When we reached the police station, we went inside and presently he took me into an office where an elderly man with grey hair sat, frowning thoughtfully. He looked up inquiringly at the policeman who nodded. Then the elderly man said: 'Dr LaSalle?'

'Yes,' I said.

'I'm the magistrate here,' he explained. 'My name is Kenicott. I'm glad to know you.'

'Thank you.' We shook hands.

He said: 'I'm sorry about this thing but it can't be helped. It's probably the best for all of us.'

'I don't understand you.'

'That was a damned fine thing,' he said. 'It took a lot of courage to do it. I'm glad you made it safely.' He shook his head sadly. 'I don't like to have to push you off like this.'

'I don't understand you.'

'You see,' he said, 'one of my men picked up Louis

I stared. 'He did?'

'He followed her for several blocks, so she said, and behaved most suspiciously. She was afraid that he – oh, well, she might have been falsely alarmed. In any case, she found a policeman who promptly brought Mr Benet here.'

'I see,' I said.

'A little questioning,' he explained, 'brought out the fact that he was one of the crew which recently escaped from the Guiana. . . . Again, congratulations. I admire your pluck. . . . He told me that I should get in touch with you and he told me where you might be.'

'Why me?'

'You see, Doctor,' Kennicott's voice rumbled now, 'I cannot release this man on his own. He has acted much too suspiciously. Learning, however, that he was a member of your party, I decided, after a consultation with the governor, to inform you of his decision in the matter.'

'I see,' I said. 'And that is?'

'I regret to inform you that the governor says you must leave the island within twenty-four hours. You understand why, of course. If you are still in Port of Spain when the twenty-four hours are up, it will be my painful duty to place you all under arrest and to hold you, pending extradition proceedings.'

'I see,' I said.

'I'm damned sorry,' he said apologetically.

'I guess there's nothing you can do.'

'Frankly, there isn't.'

'It's decent of the governor to give us twenty-four hours anyway,' I said. 'The men will appreciate that.'

Kennicott sighed. 'It hurts me to send you out again. Mr Benet mentioned an open boat and a storm. You have lost three men?'

'Yes.'

'I wish you good luck on the next leg,' he said. 'And I'm sorry. Know that.'

'Thank you,' I said.

'Mr Benet,' he said, 'will be held incommunicado until you are ready to sail. You can get him then.'

'Yes. All right,' I replied. 'I'll do that.'

Kennicott said: 'Well, Doctor, thank you for your co-operation. I must remind you again – twenty-four hours.'

'We'll be gone,' I said. 'Thanks.'

'Not at all. Good evening.'

The night was uncomfortably sticky. The heat didn't fade with the darkness as it had at sea. It clung to me heavily and my clean shirt gradually wrinkled as it soaked up perspiration.

I walked slowly back to the pier where the sloop was tied and I felt peculiarly empty all the way. I wanted to wander a little and think the whole thing over and I was glad to find the pier and the sloop deserted.

Returning to the city I strolled aimlessly around the streets. Once I stopped in a tobacco store and bought a cigar. The man eyed me with interest when I paid in francs, and he showed a marked tendency to be conversational, but I left as quickly as I could and resumed my trek. I smoked only two puffs of the cigar and then threw it away. I didn't like it at all. It didn't sicken me. I just didn't like it. It didn't feel right to be doing it. I thought I might run into one of the other men and I hoped it would be Cambreau because I wanted to see him and talk to him alone about Benet and myself. But I didn't see any of them then. I did find Roy Meredith again.

I was going past the entrance to a hotel when he came running out and nearly ran into me. He stopped and grinned, holding back some secret excitement.

'Hello there, LaSalle!' he exclaimed.

'Hello,' I said. 'I'm glad to see you again.'

'Seeing the fair city?' he asked.

'Not so much,' I said. 'I've just been walking. I felt rather lonely. None of the others has put in an appearance yet.'

'Oh,' he said, puzzling, 'anything new?'

'Yes, we're leaving tomorrow by order of the governor.'

'You are?' he asked. 'When did you find that out?'

'Half hour ago,' I replied. 'One of our men ran into the police and they learned of our arrival. They got in touch with me and I was told that twenty-four hours was to be the duration of our stay.'

'That's a damned shame,' he said. 'I don't envy you that trip in the sloop again. It's inhuman to send you off like that. Must you take the sloop? Isn't there any other way you can get off? . . . Why don't you ship out on a regular steamer? No money?'

'It isn't a matter of money,' I said. 'I think most of us have enough money. It's the passport regulation that holds us up. And the fact that we are escaped convicts. Immigration authorities are very cool towards escaped convicts. Extradition treaties make it imperative for them to re-arrest you and hold you. They're really being very kind to us here, giving us a time-limit like that. They could just as well put us in jail and wait for the French authorities to catch up with us.'

'It's too bad,' he said. 'But don't worry about it yet. I'm seeing my American gang tonight. They're always full of ideas. I'll see what they can do. Where will you head?'

'I don't know,' I replied.

'Tell you why I asked,' he said. 'I cabled my office this afternoon and asked for the assignment to follow you wherever you're going.'

'Why not come with us?' I asked dryly.

'No thanks,' he made a face. 'If you don't mind, I'll fly to your destination and wait for you. I don't like open boats and I get seasick when I look at drinking water. . . . By the way, that Cambreau chap you spoke about –'

'Yes?'

'It interested me. There's something wrong, you know. He should be in the list. I cabled the French

109

offices in the Guiana for some data on him.'

I frowned.

'Don't worry,' he assured me. 'They won't catch up with you. I just made it a pertinent question. Did a Cambreau escape from the colony? And I signed the cable address Trinidad. It won't tip them off that you're here and I won't get an answer until after you're gone anyhow. . . . Listen, LaSalle, I'm sorry as hell but I've got to beat it. One of the local reporters just tipped me off there's a good show going on over in the Negro quarter of the town. Some sort of a miracle-man stuff. A guy is supposed to have healed a lame kid. Made him throw away his crutches. The rumour got around fast and now there's a mob scene. Everybody is trying to get to the guy to be healed or something or other. You know how niggers are for religion. They say he's Jesus Christ come back again.' He laughed. 'What a break! They teach you in journalism schools that the biggest news story that can ever break is the second coming of Christ. . . . And here I am right on the scene!'

'Is that so?' I asked, 'about the healing?'

'Sure. At least that's the rumour. I just heard it inside. There's a porter babbling all over the place. Says he saw it with his own eyes.'

'Would you mind?' I said. 'I'd like to come along.'

'Okeh by me,' Meredith laughed again. 'But don't come on the chance that it's the second coming. I doubt if the Lord would pick the nigger section of Port of Spain for the debut.'

'There is no reason why he wouldn't,' I said. 'But it's not that. It's the healing.'

'Sure,' he said. 'Come along. Glad to have you.'

When we got there, an hysterical mob of Negroes was milling in the street, some shouting, some laughing, some crying. We got out of the cab and mingled among them. Meredith finally snared one fellow who seemed less agitated than the others and asked: 'Is this where the healer is supposed to be?'

'Yes, sir,' the Negro said. 'But he isn't here now. He's gone, sir. They frightened him away.'

'Frightened him?' I said.

'Well, they didn't exactly frighten him, but when the good word got around, there was more people than he could handle.'

He spoke plain English, without any accent.

'Well, tell me,' Meredith inquired, 'what happened? Did you see it all?'

'Yes, sir, I sure did. I saw the whole thing. I was standing right here on the corner with Lewis. We were talking and smoking when it all happened and we saw the whole thing.'

'What's your name?' Meredith asked, taking out a pencil and a sheaf of paper.

'James Wilson,' he answered. 'What is it, sir?'

'I'm a newspaper man,' Meredith told him. 'I just want the story, that's all. Tell me exactly what happened?'

'Well, sir,' the Negro explained, 'I was standing here with John Lewis and we were talking. It was hot and some of the children were playing in the street there. One of them, Daniel Lynn – he's Will Lynn's only son – was watching the children play. Danny's been lame all his life. He was born with one leg shorter than the other one and he had to use crutches to get around. . . . Well, sir, we were standing here when all of a sudden, I saw two gentlemen come walking down the street.'

'White?' Meredith asked.

'Yes, sir,' said Wilson, 'they were white men. They came right down the street. One of them – not the man who healed – scared Danny Lynn who started to edge away. This man did give you quite a turn. He didn't have a hair on his head and it made him look kind of horrid. . . . Well, sir, as soon as Danny started edging away, the other gentleman reached out and touched him and then

111

he said: Don't be frightened, Daniel. This man won't hurt you. And you know I won't hurt you, don't you? Just like that he said it.'

Meredith was puzzled. 'But how did he know the kid's name?'

'He knew it,' Wilson said. 'Praise God he knew it. He knew everything. He was the Lord Jesus himself!'

'Well go on,' Meredith said dubiously. 'What then?'

'Then Danny said: I'm not afraid of *you* sir, he said, and he looked at the man without any hair and said: I'm sorry for being afraid of you, sir. And they all just stood there for a second. The children in the street stopped playing and they were watching the hairless man. He was a sight to see, without any hair like that. Well, sir, the Lord Jesus said then: Danny, you're a good boy, aren't you? And Danny said: Yes, sir, I am. And the Lord Jesus said: You'd like to run and play like your young friends, wouldn't you? And Danny looked kind of sad and said: I would, sir, but I can't. I'm lame. Then the Lord Jesus laughed. He laughed a long time and it sounded pretty and soon he had Danny laughing and all the other children laughing. Then we all started to laugh. And all of a sudden, he stopped laughing and we all stopped and then his voice came out loud and clear and he said: Danny, do you believe in God? And Danny said right back just as clear: Yes, sir, I do. And the Lord Jesus said: Did God make you lame? And Danny looked kind of surprised and said: Oh, no, sir. God wouldn't make anyone lame. *You* know that sir. *You* know that God is good and so do *I*. Just like that he said it. Then the Lord Jesus smiled and said: Then throw away your crutches, Danny, and play with your friends. And Danny – I swear this, gentlemen – threw away his crutches and ran and jumped and his legs were as strong as any man's!'

Meredith glanced at me and whispered: 'This man is on the level. I think he's telling the truth.'

'I know he is,' I replied.

Meredith frowned at me. Then he turned back to the Negro and asked: 'What did they look like, what did these two men look like?'

'I told you,' Wilson said. 'The one man, he didn't have any hair on his head at all. He was wearing a nice clean pair of white pants. He just stood there and watched the whole thing and he smiled all the time after Danny said he wasn't afraid.'

'But what did the healer look like?'

'He was the Lord Jesus come back,' Wilson exclaimed fervently. 'Praise God, he was that.'

'But what did he *look* like?' Meredith asked.

'I couldn't say, sir, as how he looked at all. You couldn't describe him. I don't know as how he was tall or short or light or dark. I just know he was white. He had eyes and a voice. I remember those. His voice was loud and clear and his eyes kind of sparkled with something that made you feel good all inside.'

Meredith rubbed his chin thoughtfully. He was impressed. 'What happened after that?' he asked.

'Well, sir,' Wilson continued, 'I saw the whole thing. As soon as Danny ran off home to his father, old Mary Walker came over to him and touched him. She'd seen the whole thing too. And she said to him: Lord Jesus, heal me. Now Mary Walker is nearly seventy-five years old and she'd lost the sight in her left eye and was blind in that eye for the last eight years. And when she touched him and said: Lord Jesus, heal me, he turned to her and smiled at her and said: We see from within, Mary, not from without. And seeing from within, your eye cannot be imperfect at all because you never saw with it in the beginning. You always saw from your heart. And he placed his hand over her eye and took it away and she fell down on her knees in front of him and said: I can see with it again! God Bless you! God bless you! And he said: God *has* blessed me. He has blessed us all. You cannot ask for something which you already have.'

113

The Negro paused. Meredith's eyes were shining. He was completely absorbed in the story. 'Go on,' he said.

'Well, sir,' Wilson continued, 'the good word spread like fire and people began to crowd around him and ask to be healed of their ailments and there was shouting started up like: Jesus Christ is come again and All hail the Lord Jesus. Then he held up his hand and he said: I cannot heal you all. You must do that yourselves. There is nothing which I have done that you cannot do yourselves. And the people got down in front of him and said: But we don't know what to do. We don't understand. And he said: Go to that boy. Go to Daniel and ask him. For he was more understanding than all of you together.'

'Go on,' Meredith said. 'What happened then?'

Wilson shrugged. 'Then he just disappeared down the street with the hairless man and although the crowd followed him a way, he disappeared all of a sudden and he was gone.'

Later, after Meredith had corroborated Wilson's story by interviewing others who had seen it, he found the facts to be exactly the same. When we rode back to the hotel in a cab, Meredith was profoundly thoughtful. He said: 'It gets me, LaSalle. Those people couldn't all have been hypnotized. There were two miracles down there to-night.'

'I know,' I said.

'It makes me feel queer.'

'Why?' I asked.

'Well,' he said, 'you remember I joked with you about the second coming. I'm wondering now whether or not . . .'

'No,' I said. 'If you are thinking that Jesus materialized down there to-night, forget it. He didn't.'

'Something materialized,' he said. 'There was a man.'

'Two men,' I said. 'Neither of them was the Christ.'

He stared at me.

'How do you know that?'

I shrugged. 'I just know it.'

'But how?'

'I just know it.' I fingered the empty space on the bridge of my nose where my glasses had rested for thirty years and I smiled.

'Well,' Meredith sighed, 'it sure beats me. I guess the day of miracles isn't past.' He hit his knee forcefully. 'It must have been beautiful to see! I wish I'd been there!'

I left him at the hotel. When he said goodbye, he told me that he would see me at the pier in the morning. He was a nice young fellow. I liked him.

5

When I got back to the boat I found Weiner sitting on the pier, and Flaubert and Cambreau down in the boat. Flaubert was asleep. He had on a new shirt and pair of white ducks that were dirty from the bilge. He snored. Weiner was holding his chin in his hands and looking down at the logs until he saw me. Then he said: 'Well, look who's here.'

'Hello,' I said.

Cambreau greeted me cheerfully: 'Hello, Doctor!'

'God-damn,' Weiner said, 'if you aren't dressed fit to kill!' He laughed. 'Where did you get the outfit?'

'I bought it.'

'Well, God Almighty,' he said, 'you sure look like the Beau Brummel of the south seas. You and the crazy bug. He looks pretty good too.' I noticed that Weiner was wearing his same clothes, grey pants, grey shirt. Cambreau had the same clothes too, only his looked clean and they weren't torn.

'I've got some bad news,' I said, climbing down into the boat and sitting opposite Cambreau.

Weiner sighed. 'I knew I liked this place too damn much. What is it?'

Cambreau looked at me. 'We can't stay,' he said.

'What?' Weiner exclaimed.

'That's it,' I said. 'We can't stay.'

'What the hell do you mean?'

'We can't stay, we've got to get out of here. We've got to sail inside of twenty-four hours or we'll be arrested and held for extradition.'

Weiner stared, then spit against the pier.

116

I said softly to Cambreau: 'You knew this would happen.'

'Yes,' he said.

'Where are we going next?' I asked.

'Santiago de Cuba,' he said.

'Will we all make it?' I asked.

'All of us?' he said. 'Yes.'

'And then where?' I asked.

'Florida,' he said. 'But all of us won't make there.'

'God-damn it!' Weiner said. 'I don't understand this at all! How did the police find out we were here? Where'd they get wind of that anyhow?'

'Benet told them,' I said. 'He's in jail.'

Weiner slapped his cheek. 'In jail? For God's sake, why?'

'He followed a woman.'

That shocked Weiner; I don't know why but it did. He had teased Benet about the thing often enough but when he found out that Benet had really made another try within a few hours after landing, it shocked him. I could see the whiteness of his face. He didn't say a word. His eyes popped, sort of, and he held his face in his hands and stared straight ahead.

The sloop rocked gently with the tide. It was nearly level with the pier now because the tide had come in. Cambreau kept looking at me and smiling. Finally I said: 'There's a rumour around the coloured quarters that Jesus Christ came back to-night.'

'It's false,' he smiled.

'I know,' I said. I paused a long time. 'For a while I though you might be he.'

'That's ridiculous,' he said. 'Why do you say that?'

I shrugged.

'You healed my eyes,' I said. 'You healed that boy's leg. You healed that woman's blindness.'

'That's nothing at all,' he said. 'That isn't half of what I can do. That isn't half of what *you* can do.'

'You mean I could have healed that boy too?'

'Of course you could have.'

'But how?'

'Well,' he said, 'that's hard to explain. You would have had to have seen him perfect instead of lame. You would have had to know that real as lameness was to him, it was an illusion of his own belief, that it wasn't real. When you knew that and knew *why* it wasn't real, you could have healed him.'

'But how can I do that?' I asked. 'I'm only a man.'

'So am I,' he said.

'But you're different,' I said.

'No, I'm not. I'm not different at all.'

'But everything you do is right, everything is perfect.'

'It should be,' he said. 'In doing it all for some one else. I never can fail. You see, God is right behind me. When I lose sight of him for only an instant, he nudges me.'

'I envy you.'

'I know,' he said. 'But that won't be for long. You're going to live a beautiful life, Doctor.'

'Tell me about it,' I asked.

'You're going to wander. You're going to go from place to place and you're going to bring perfection unto everyone whom you meet. You're going to heal and you'll always be anonymous because you won't want to dazzle people.'

'I'm going to do that?'

'Very soon.'

'I want to,' I said fervently. 'Help me to do that.'

He sighed. 'How quickly you progress! I told you once that all you had to do was ask for something and you'd have it. You've asked. I warn you, you will never be the same again. You will look on our civilization as something strange and foreign, all of it. You'll be sad when you see where it stands, but you'll recognize a lone spark in it, a tiny spark that needs fanning, and you'll fan it and soon the spark will flame and spread. It will take centuries, but

118

it will spread and some day – the new civilization will come.'

Later Pennington returned, crestfallen. He climbed down into the yawl. 'No luck,' he announced. 'I didn't have enough money. They wouldn't have taken me anyway.'

'That's too bad,' I said. 'We have to sail again tomorrow.' And I told him the whole story about Benet.

Telez returned too. He seemed in better spirits, but he did not mind the sailing ultimatum at all. 'So much the better,' he said in Spanish, 'I have a cousin in Santiago de Cuba. Let us go there.'

6

When I awakened next morning, Roy Meredith was
standing on the pier calling to me. I felt inclined to
sleep. I had the loginess in the body and the heaviness
in the eyelids, but a certain excitement in his voice
pervaded me. I got up reluctantly and splashed some
sea water on my face to bring me out of it. My white
trousers and coat were all wrinkled and soiled from the
sleep in the sloop, but I didn't mind much. I climbed up
on to the pier. The tide had receded again and the
sloop floated low.

I saw that Cambreau and Flaubert were gone as was
Pennington; DuFond was not there either. Telez sat in the
boat. He was cleaning his finger nails carefully. Weiner
sat up on the piling, his uncombed hair erect.

'Hello,' I said to Meredith, 'how are you?'

'Hello!' he shook my hand. 'Swell news for you!'

'Really?'

'The sloop is out,' he said. 'Done for, finished. You
won't have to sail in it!'

'What do you mean?' I asked, rubbing my eyes.

'Just that!' he said. 'You remember my American
gang? I told you about them last night. Well, I told them
the whole damn story and they went to bat. They said it
was a crying shame to have you men put off like that into
the open sea on a scow like this where your chances of
making another port were nothing short of zero-zero. So
they did something!'

'What?'

'They bought you a ship, a 38-foot schooner!'

I stared.

Weiner got up and came over. 'Say, who the hell is this man?'

'My name's Meredith.'

'This is Carl Weiner,' I said. 'He's one of the crew. Meredith is an American reporter.'

'Never mind that,' Weiner said. 'What's this other stuff?' He squinted. 'Are you on the level?'

'You bet I am,' Meredith assured him. 'I'm giving it to you straight. The gang bought you a schooner. It's not particularly elegant. We picked it up from one of the fishermen. But it's seaworthy and it's got an auxiliary engine and eight bunks and there's a galley.'

'God Almighty!' Weiner breathed hard.

'She's a good ship,' Meredith said. 'You could sail her around the world safe and sound. She's got a round belly and an eight-foot keel.'

'But –'

'She's solid as iron. Her name is the *Albatross*. Say, she's even registered at Lloyds! She's a *ship!* What do you think of that?'

'Think of it?' I asked. 'How did you ever do it?'

'Oh, well –'

'She must have cost a fortune!'

'No she didn't. We picked her up for a song. The fellow was saving to get a larger boat anyhow and he was just as anxious to get rid of this one as we were to buy it. We just tore her all to pieces, said she would sink in a bathtub and we finally got him believing it.'

'But a 38-foot schooner!' I exclaimed.

'That'll get you where you want to go,' he said.

'God Almighty!' Weiner shouted. 'Hey, Jesus, hear that? Did you hear what this man said?'

'*Si,*' Telez replied. His black eyes were shining and he was standing in the boat below.

'Where is she?' Weiner said. 'Where the hell is this ocean liner? Lead me to her, mister!'

'She's down the waterfront about half a mile,' Meredith said.

121

'We'll have to stock her,' I exclaimed suddenly. 'Where did the other men go? We've got to get food and water aboard her. And we've got to get out of here soon. The sooner the better. We can't take any chances on the governor's changing his mind.'

'God Almighty,' Weiner said. 'I can't believe it!'

Meredith smiled and shook his head. 'It's true all right. And you don't have to stock her. She's stocked. We arranged all that. We got the food much cheaper than you could have. And the water tank is loaded up to the nozzle. You're stocked for a month at sea, LaSalle. You haven't a thing to worry about.'

'Say,' Weiner asked suspiciously, 'what are you getting out of this anyhow?'

'Getting?' Meredith said, surprised. 'I'm not getting anything.'

'Why are you doing it then?' Weiner asked.

'To help you men out, that's all. To give you a chance of making safety. You wouldn't have much of a one in that open boat.'

'You mean you're just doing this to help us?' Weiner asked, flabbergasted. 'You're not getting a thing out of it?'

'Of course not,' Meredith replied. 'You'd do the same for me.'

Weiner shook his head doubtfully.

'Sure you would, if you could.'

'I'm not so sure.'

We left Telez at the sloop to tell the others and then we went up the waterfront until we found the schooner. She was moored at a pier with lots of other schooners and some beautiful cruisers. She was in a regular slip, stern first, gently rolling with the tide. She was a beauty. Her sides were covered with flaked paint but they had wide strong curves and you could tell there wasn't a sea which she couldn't weather. She didn't look so big. She carried a mainsail, foresail, forestaysail, foretopsail, and a flying jib. We went on board and inspected her and she got in our blood so much we wanted to get going right away.

About fifteen minutes later, Pennington arrived and when he went aboard he got as excited as we were. At noon, the rest of them came with Telez, Cambreau, Flaubert, DuFond. We decided to depart. I went over to police headquarters and brought back Benet. He sulked all the way and didn't say a word. I didn't say anything to him either.

We set forth early in the afternoon. Only Meredith saw us off. 'Santiago de Cuba,' I told him when we left.

'We'll see you there?' I asked.

'You bet you will,' he answered. 'Bon voyage!'

'Thanks a thousand times,' I said.

'A million times,' Weiner added.

As we went out into the Bay of Paria he couldn't get used to the idea at all. 'I don't understand it,' he kept repeating. 'He didn't get anything out of it. He just did it to give us a break. I never heard of a man doing that before. It's not natural. He didn't get anything out of it, yet he went ahead and got us this boat just the same.'

It impressed me how that simple fact changed Weiner.

Cambreau sat by the wheel, his eyes closed, and I thought back to that first day on the beach when we awoke in the morning to learn from him that the sloop was afloat.

The boat looked inhumanly small. 'Don't worry about that. . . . We'll have a larger one after we reach Port of Spain.'

Well, we'd reached Port of Spain and we had a larger boat, all right.

I never heard Weiner swear again.

7

Next evening, when the sun dipped, we passed off the east coast of Blanquilla, an island in the lesser Antilles group. This showed how accurate the ship's compass was. We had had a fresh breeze all the way from the Dragon's Mouth exit of the Bay of Paria. It heeled us a little but not nearly as much as it had in the sloop. The spars creaked and the canvas stretched tight as we rapidly pencilled a path across the sea. The ripples of our wake made small swells themselves that spread out like the sides of a fan, while behind us in straight lines running parallel to each other and separated by the same width as our own beam, white air bubbles floated for a long time before bursting. The quietude of this voyage had a soothing effect. The sun stayed with us, but now we had a cabin so that we could go below and lie in our bunks, or we could sit in the shadow of the sail. There was no necessity of getting sunburned and there was no necessity of skimping on food and drink. We ate heartily and enjoyed it. There was little dissension. Pennington cooked and DuFond helped. Pennington really liked the job. He was always fixing new dishes and he did a fine job.

8

The fifth day, as I was sitting at the wheel, Weiner sat down beside me and said: 'I think there's a squall coming up. You can see it in the northeast, Doctor.'

I looked at the northeast and saw dark clouds racing down on us before a fast wind. They were travelling rapidly and the sky began to darken.

I looked forward and saw Telez and DuFond up in the bow. Telez was stretched out comfortably on his back and DuFond was playing with a coil of rope. The others were below.

I called to Telez and told him to get below. DuFond got up too, looking frightened, and hastily went down.

'What are you going to do?' Weiner asked.

'Why,' I said, 'we'll just have to lash the wheel and go to the cabins. There's no protection on the deck here. We might be swept overboard.'

'You've got to furl the sails,' Weiner said. 'They'll blow out when that thing hits them.'

I hadn't thought of that at all so I lashed the helm and he and I went forward, lowered the foresail and furled it. The squall was coming more rapidly than I thought. We got the mainsail down and furled it, too, tying the boom into the crotch, and then went forward again, but there was no time to furl the jib properly.

'Go below,' I ordered Weiner.

'No,' he said. 'You can't leave the helm like that. We're in the steamship lanes now. You've got to stay at the helm.'

'All right,' I said. 'I'll stay at the helm.'

'No,' he said, 'I will. You get below. I'll rope myself here so that I won't be swept over board.'

'I'll do it,' I said. I didn't want to but it was my turn and I didn't like to quit.

'You can't do that,' Weiner said. 'You're in no shape to fight the wheel. You'll hurt yourself with your rupture and everything. I'll do it. I can handle it all right.'

'That doesn't sound like you,' I said.

'Yes, it does,' he said. 'I'll handle the helm. That's me all over.'

'All right,' I said.

I gave him the wheel and watched him rope himself to the guard-rail astern so that he couldn't be swept overboard. The wind whined through the rigging. You could hear the solid creaking of the planks. Rain came from the north. You could see it sweep across the sea towards you, a thick opaque grey veil and the sea suddenly became turbulent.

'Listen!' Weiner shouted to make himself heard. 'Go below and start the engine. Full speed ahead. We've got to keep some headway in this or we'll be swamped!'

'All right,' I said.

I went below and closed the hatch securely, leaving him all alone out there. I started the engine and it functioned perfectly. It stopped the yawing sensation and the crazy rolling and we began to move. The ship vibrated with the engine. We plunged nose down, stern up, stern down, nose up, but we didn't roll as much and the crests did not swamp the stern. Weiner was right. He was getting to be a regular sailor.

Pennington had shut the cupboards tight so that the crockery was safe. I could hear the pots and pans rattling noisily in the galley. The lamps overhead swayed to and fro. DuFond lay in his bunk. He stared straight up at the lamp and with each motion of the boat, his white hands gripped the side of the bunk and the knuckles gleamed brilliantly in the half-darkness. Flaubert wept. Telez assumed his usual attitude of sullen dislike for the whole thing. He lay flat so that he could not toss around. I climbed into my bunk and stared out of a porthole. The sea was furious. The waves would hit the porthole, blot out everything and then the water would run down and away, making the scene hazy and soft. Heavy weather all right. '. . . *Poor Rudolph!* . . .' I felt sorry for Flaubert. It was too real for him. His heartracking sobs were plainly audible above the groaning of the ship's timbers.

Cambreau slept through it all.

It was only a prolonged squall that lasted six hours. Night fell before the wind suddenly stopped moaning and the sea began to subside.

When we had ceased pitching and it became possible to walk about safely, I said to Pennington: 'Make some hot coffee and hurry it. Weiner's been up there all through this. He'll need it.'

'I will,' Pennington said, and he went to the galley.

I cut the engine to half speed and then I slid open the hatch and went out on deck.

The heavy rain and the moonless night made the stern so black. I couldn't see anything, not even the breaking phosphorescence of the whitecaps. Feeling my way through the darkness and gripping the railing of the cockpit, pretty soon I felt the helm. The rain was soaking me to the skin but I didn't mind at all. I felt around the wheel, but I couldn't find Weiner's hands. Then I felt the rope. He had lashed the helm with rope guides to hold a course and his hands were gone. Frightened, I plunged recklessly around the wheel. Dangerous crests broke over the stern.

I found his right hand first. It was icy. He was lying on his back behind the helm, cold and utterly stiff. I felt for the ropes around his body and caught hold of them but I couldn't untie them because the sea had wet the knots and the strain had made them tight as steel.

Leaving him hurriedly I ran down into the cabin and got a knife from Pennington in the galley.

My face alarmed him. 'What's happened?'

127

'Weiner,' I gasped, 'I think he's dead.' I went out again and cut the ropes from his body. I struggled with his dead weight bracing myself on the helm and finally lifted him over my shoulder. I staggered back to the hatch and then slid down the companionway with Weiner. Nobody helped me. Pennington offered to, but he couldn't leave a lighted flame with the boat still pitching. I took Weiner forward. Telez, DuFond, Benet and Flaubert just stared at me. Not one of them got up to help. They just stared. Cambreau was still asleep. I laid Weiner on his bunk and stripped off his wet clothes. I never felt flesh so cold. His eyes were half-open, the pupils dilated. He looked dead. I felt his pulse and couldn't catch it at all. But he was still breathing, a mirror showed that. I didn't know whether he was drowning from water in his lungs or dying from sheer exhaustion. He didn't move. Pennington entered with the coffee. I took a little of it and tried to pour some down his throat, but decided not to because he was completely unconscious and his throat muscles didn't work at all. I might have choked him to death. I put all the blankets I could over him to make him warm. Then I sat beside him and waited for him to do something, but he didn't move. Pennington came over and sat beside me. 'I'm afraid of that, Doctor,' he said. 'He looks dead.' 'He's not dead,' I said. 'He's breathing.' But breathing didn't mean a thing. His skin was like wax. He looked dead, breathing or no breathing.

9

We kept the helm lashed and the sails furled and I cut the engine and let it die. We drifted. The waters had calmed and the schooner rolled gently like a cradle. The rain continued and the sounds of the drops against the surface of the sea had an hypnotic monotony.

After a while, I left Pennington with Weiner and took Telez with me. We went up on deck in the rain and hoisted the foresail. I saw the jib had flown out. The wind had lulled, but it was strong enough to fill the foresail with a dull crack and we moved forward again. I didn't want to drift for fear we might lose our bearings altogether. When we had set the foresail and laid a course by the compass, I went below again leaving Telez at the helm and closing the hatch so that the rain could not come in. It was pouring and I was wet through. The cabin was hot, too hot. I opened a porthole and went back to Weiner.

Flaubert was snoring. He had cried himself to sleep. DuFond was asleep too.

Weiner had not changed at all, except that his eyes had closed, cutting off the stony stare. That made me feel better. I didn't like the glassiness of the eyes. I felt for his pulse and I still couldn't find it, but when I tried the mirror, I found he was still breathing. His flesh was cold, his lips white.

Pennington yawned and tried to stay awake, but seeing that he was dog-tired I said: 'I'll sit up with him. You get some sleep.'

'I don't like to leave you alone,' Pennington said.

'That's all right,' I replied. 'I'll wake you up if he comes to. You'll fall asleep if you sit here.'

He smiled. 'Guess I would at that. All right, I'll turn in. Wake me up if you want a little relief.'

'I will,' I said.

He got up and then turned back again. 'How would you like some coffee? That might help.'

I nodded. 'Thanks.'

He went to the galley and came back with a cup of coffee. It made me feel much better.

After Pennington turned in, it was very still. There were sounds, the swishing waves, the creaking of the masts, the squeak of the lantern handle where it swung from a nail in the overhead planking, Flaubert's resonant snore, the whisper of the raindrops on the sea, the sound of the wind whistling past the open porthole, the dull thud of the bow when it nosed down into each wave, but in spite of all this the silence was heavy. All those little noises, rolled together, produced the effect of silence. I was too used to them to hear them.

The coffee didn't do me much good. My eyelids drooped. I fought to keep awake but it was hopeless. I remember glancing at Weiner while the swinging lantern cast a yellowish glow on his face. He looked waxy, as much like a corpse as any one I'd ever seen.

Then I dozed.

It seemed I had been sleeping soundly a long time there, sitting beside his bunk, when I dreamed I was up on deck in the rain, standing at the helm and peering into the night. The sea was rough and the foresail wasn't drawing as the schooner tossed. I had to wrestle with the wheel all the time and I was tired of it. I was alone: none of the other men was anywhere around. Presently the rain turned into a heavy mist that settled close to the water. I never felt so utterly lonely. I stood there, peering until red spots danced before my eyes. Then suddenly out of the night came the belch of a foghorn that sent a violent chill down my back. I looked around in a panic. Again the horn blasted almost in my ears. I looked to port and I shrieked. The huge black bow of an ocean liner pierced the fog, coming towards the schooner as though to cut it in two. . . .

At that moment I awakened, my face dripping with sweat, and as I opened my eyes I could almost swear that the echo of that fog-horn still reverberated dully in my ears. It was so real that I got up and ran to the hatch which I found open. Looking back I saw Telez lying in his bunk. I climbed out on to the stern where Cambreau was sitting at the wheel.

Over his shoulder, not twenty feet away, the black bulk of a ship was passing swiftly, its twinkling myriad lights hazily visible.

'I knew it,' I said hoarsely.

Cambreau smiled.

'Did you?' he asked.

'I dreamed it!' I said. 'I just dreamed it!'

He seemed amused. 'How is Weiner?' he asked.

'I don't know,' I said, bracing myself against the sway as I watched the stern of the liner pass into the mist and disappear. 'The last time I looked at him he could have been dead.'

'Go and see,' he said.

Still panting at the near-collision, I went downstairs and examined Weiner. Telez roused himself and asked anxiously: 'What was that sound?'

'A liner,' I said. 'It just missed us.'

'*Dios mio,*' he said. 'It frightened me.'

I couldn't tell whether Weiner was dead or alive. I couldn't find any breathing this time. I couldn't find any pulse. That was enough to make him dead. But when I looked at his eyes, I saw that the pupils had contracted and that raised doubts. I went on deck again and told Cambreau.

He said: 'Well, now, you're a medico, aren't you? Why don't you do something for him?'

'I can't,' I said.

'Why not?' he asked.

'I can't do anything,' I explained, 'I haven't any stimulants, no hypo needle, nothing. I can't do any-thing.'

'You lead me to believe,' he said, 'that the human treatment of pathology is inadequate. Must you always have your scalpels and your needles and medicines?'

'Of course. Doctors can't work miracles.'

'You mean doctors cannot heal.'

I didn't say anything.

'They can treat,' he said. 'But they cannot heal. Take away their medicines and what can they do? Take away their scalpels and where is their surgery?'

I said: 'I can't do anything for him! Don't you understand –'

'Of course I do,' he interrupted. 'Take the wheel. I want to show you something.'

I took the wheel and he went below. After a few minutes, Telez came out of the cabin a little wildeyed. *'Maria Santisima,'* he gasped. 'That man is a devil!'

'What's the matter?' I asked.

'That man,' Telez shivered and rubbed his shoulders. 'He came down and he went over to Weiner and he said: Hello, Weiner, wake up there. And Weiner opened his eyes and sat up!' He crossed himself fervently and opened his mouth to speak again when Cambreau came up from below. Telez choked off his words and went forward, unmindful of the rain.

'Hello!' Cambreau said cheerfully.

'What have you done now?' I asked.

'Something,' he said dryly, 'which a doctor could not do.'

Weiner poked his head out of the hatch and grinned at me. 'I'm all right, Doctor. Did I scare you? . . . I'm sorry.' And he disappeared below.

We sat there for a long time in silence. Avoiding Cambreau's eyes I stared straight ahead, although I couldn't see a thing in the fog. Presently Telez stole back to the stern and fled down into the cabin, muttering darkly to himself as he avoided Cambreau who seemed amused. I could hear him chuckle.

There were just the two of us then.

'Well? . . .'

'I want to know,' I pleaded. 'I want to learn.'

'It's your life.'

'I know it is.'

'It will taste sweet at first; but it will gall you later.'

'What did you say?'

'It will taste sweet at first; but it will gall you later.'

And the voice which I heard from heaven spake unto me again and said, Go and take the little book which is open in the hand of the angel which standeth upon the sea and upon the earth. And I went unto the angel, and said unto him, Give me the little book. And he said unto me, Take it, and eat it up; and it shall make thy belly bitter, but it shall be in thy mouth sweet as honey. And I took the little book out of the angel's hand, and ate it up; and it was in my mouth sweet as honey: and as soon as I had eaten it, my belly was bitter. And he said unto me, Thou must prophesy again before many people, and nations, and tongues, and kings.

Cambreau said: 'Here, Philip.'

He handed me Moll's dilapidated Bible. 'I have marked a certain book. There are many other books in this book but none of them can teach you any more than this particular one. It explains you to yourself and others to you. This hypothesis was proven by the man who practised it. . . . That was long ago and you are human enough, perhaps, to have doubted that demonstration. Human because the demonstration itself was *humanly* impossible.'

'I know,' I said. 'That's why you healed my eyes. That's why you prophesied. That's why you brought back Weiner. . . .'

'Is that all?' Cambreau asked – 'Only those?'

133

'Was there something more?'

He laughed.

'Tonight,' he said, 'you carried Weiner from here to the cabin. He weighed one hundred and eighty pounds and you weigh one hundred and forty-five and you were suffering from the delusion of a ruptured hernia. . . . Is that humanly possible?'

I couldn't reply.

'You see, Philip, your truss is gone. It has been gone for two days and you have been very blind not to have noticed. You were blind tonight when you saw Weiner as a dying man. You have been blind all along when you saw Pennington as the inevitable victim of a disease.'

'Yes?' I said.

'I have healed you twice,' he said. 'Your eyes and your groin. I showed you to-night the fallacy of your own senses. I will show you in the future, the fallacy of human law. Pennington will not die. He'll live.'

'Yes?' I asked again.

'This is a new order, Philip. From to-night on, you are changed. Now you have a grain of faith and a grain of understanding.'

'Yes?'

'The designated book will teach you how. Read it once and see the words. Read it twice and understand them. Read it three times – and practise.'

'Yes?'

'Good night,' Cambreau said, smiling. 'God blesses you.'

10

On the eighth afternoon at sea, the wind died, and Flaubert found a revolver.

It was shortly past noon and we were beating northwest at six knots when we suddenly ran into a pocket and all motion ceased. There was no breath of wind at all and the sun quickly became hot. The sails sagged limply not even fluttering. The sea was glassy and if you looked at it hard and long enough, you could almost imagine you saw steam rising from the waveless surface. The swells were so gentle, they gave the schooner no roll at all. I was sitting at the wheel with Weiner beside me when the calm fell and I didn't know what to do. The use of the engine during the storm had sapped the petrol supply and I did not want to use it again unless I had to. I thought it would be better if we reserved our fuel in case some emergency arose.

DuFond was standing on the forward deck, holding one of the foresail halyards with one arm as he watched the horizon. Telez sat with his back against the mast, the shadow of the sail covering his body. He had pulled his knees way up and his chin rested on them as he stared moodily at the water. Benet, Pennington, Cambreau and Flaubert were below.

'The wind's died,' I said.

'It will come up again,' Weiner remarked without turning. 'Just hold the wheel and you'll see.'

'All right,' I said.

We sat there quietly, feeling the placidness of the scene. Presently the sound of a motor broke the stillness and we all looked around. Off to the south, we made out the black speck of an aeroplane, flying west.

'Look at that,' Weiner said. 'Isn't it funny how you can hear the sound? He's pretty far off.'

'It's a Clipper ship,' I said. 'Probably flying up from Trinidad.'

Weiner shook his head. 'Think of that. He'll be in Havana to-night.'

'Not quite,' I said. 'Probably Port au Prince. Havana is quite a jump. It's only two hours from Miami. That's still pretty far off.'

'I guess you're right. But all the same, aeroplanes are marvellous things. They're breaking down the last stand of space. . . .' He grinned. 'Though of course, if Pennington is right, space has no last stand because it doesn't exist.'

'Sharks!' DuFond shouted back.

We sat up. 'Where?'

'Right off starboard quarter,' DuFond pointed with his free hand. 'You can see the fins above the water. Watch them. There!'

'I see them.' Weiner squinted over his right shoulder. 'Are they sharks?'

'They look like porpoises,' I said. 'That's the way porpoises keep jumping up and down.'

'No,' said DuFond. 'They're not porpoises. They're not jumping up and down. They're swimming in a straight line. I can see them better here. They're sharks all right. Maneaters, I think. They look pretty nasty. Look! The fins are up now!'

They were sharks all right, swimming lazily and looking as though they would pass behind us. They were the first sharks we had seen during the whole voyage.

We were watching them swim past when I saw Flaubert come up out of the hatch and stand in front of it. I saw him only out of the corner of my eye and I didn't pay much attention to him at first because those sharks were interesting to watch. But when I heard Weiner whisper to

136

me: 'Doctor –' I turned and then I saw the thing.

Flaubert was staring at Weiner, working his lips soundlessly. He looked quite mad. He was holding a .22 calibre revolver in his right hand, one of those target guns with a long blue- steel barrel and a large steadying stock which he gripped tightly.

Weiner licked his lips nervously: 'I think –'

'Flaubert,' I ordered, 'put that gun down.'

'No.' He shook his head back and forth savagely and gripped the gun tighter. It was aimed on a line with Weiner's stomach.

'What are you trying to do,' I said; 'scare us?'

'No!' he shook his head.

'Doctor,' Weiner said hoarsely, 'I think. . . .'

'Shh!' Flaubert said. 'Don't you talk!'

'Put that gun down!' I yelled at him. 'Put it down, I say!'

'I'm going to kill him,' Flaubert said. 'He wants to kill me. He's been trying to kill poor Rudolph all the time just like he killed Dunning!'

Weiner murmured, barely audible: 'He'll do it – he's mad – I deserve this.'

'He won't hit poor Rudolph's head again! He won't hurt me any more,' Flaubert whined.

His finger looked dangerously taut on the trigger.

I glanced at Telez's set face and said quickly in Spanish so that Flaubert wouldn't understand: 'Quick, Jesus, jump him from behind there and get that gun out of his hand!'

Telez shook his head while his hands gripped the mast. 'Not me. I don't want to die.'

'I'm going to kill him,' Flaubert said.

Meanwhile DuFond's feet pattered on the deck as he ran the length of the ship. *'Flaubert! Don't do that!'*

Flaubert jerked the gun around and yelled: 'Don't you say that! Don't you come any nearer or I'll kill you too! I'll kill you all! You hate me! All of you hate poor Rudolph! I'll kill you all, every one!'

DuFond didn't stop. He dived down from the top of the cabin over the coaming right at Flaubert, who looked surprised and fired the gun into DuFond's body as they collided. There was no explosion. The hammer only clicked. Nobody looked more stunned than Flaubert. The next instant DuFond had wrested the gun out of his hand and hurled it far overboard. Flaubert stood there a second, staring at the circle of the splash, then he emitted a wail and plunged overboard.

DuFond stood by the railing, aghast, looking overboard as Flaubert rose to the surface, his head shining with water, his arms and legs flailing wildly.

The rest of us were dumbfounded.

DuFond raised his eyes outward briefly, caught his lip in his teeth, and quickly dived into the water. He came up beside Flaubert, went down again, and when he came up the second time he was behind Flaubert. With his right arm crooked around Flaubert's neck he kicked them both to the side of the schooner.

It was grim – the way those sharks scented the trouble. Weiner and I lifted Flaubert and DuFond out just as a concerted rushing and swirling of water came close to the schooner. The black dorsal fins disappeared as the sleek greyish-white upturned bellies flashed by hungrily, and then came back again.

Weiner put Flaubert over his shoulder and carried him downstairs. DuFond sat down, trembling. The water dripped from his clothes and his hair was down over his eyes. He looked tired and panted heavily.

When I could speak I said: 'That was a brave thing to do. Didn't you see those sharks?'

'I saw them,' he said, 'that's why I went in. I couldn't leave him there like that. He didn't know what he was doing.'

'That was a brave thing to do,' I said. 'It took courage.'

'I couldn't leave him there,' DuFond replied. Suddenly he looked up. 'Courage . . . ?'

'It took courage,' I repeated.

He played with the word. 'Courage, courage. . . . It did, didn't it? It did take courage, didn't it?'

'More than I have,' I said. 'Good work.'

'I couldn't –' He stopped and looked up at me. His eyes were steady and shining. 'Thanks, Doctor,' he said in strong firm tones and then he smiled broadly. It was the first time I had ever seen him smile.

11

One night we sat in the bow, Cambreau and I, and watched the beauty of the moonlight on the water. Weiner was at the helm, half-asleep, half-awake, as he steered us along the coast where – in the clear unmisted distance – the lights of Tiburon twinkled bravely in the darkness against the blacker and more majestic darkness of Cape Dame Marie where the bulky outline of the mountains rose precipitously from the floor of the sea.

The wind had pushed us steadily along our course and we were only two hundred miles from the southern edge of Cuba. The canvas billowed but no sound came from it at all.

We talked quietly for a long time up there, with the jib curved out over our heads. I had read my book. I had done everything but understand it fully. I understood what the words meant, but I could not understand what the words could do, how I could apply them. And this was what Cambreau taught me.

To him it was tedious. He knew it all. He understood the difficulty of translating it into my thought. 'Words are spirit,' he said. 'That's why it is so large a task to feel them, instead of read them. When you try to understand what is written here you must understand in your *heart* – not in your brain. For when you think about the words, you consider their human possibility and you consider their human application and you suddenly perceive that you are considering everything about them through your own senses and that they are beyond that. . . . You cannot catch them with your senses. You must catch them with your heart, with the love which you can feel, the gratitude

140

which you express, the meekness and peace that is you.'

He told me many other things too, and once he said: 'You cannot understand now how hard it is for me to make you know. Faith is not enough. Faith will sustain you, but it will not let you sustain others. You must understand the things you are going to do, and once you have understood, you can never forget them. Some day you will write down this whole experience, and when you come to the things I am telling you, your manuscript will falter and you'll struggle to write it down and you'll fail. You'll be strangely reticent about what I have told you. The things I have shown you materially, will be very clear. But the things of the spirit you will not be able to put down. They'll elude you.'

'Why will that be?' I asked.

'Because the spirit is the spirit,' he said. 'You cannot describe it. You only feel it. And you do not feel as you might feel the illusion of pain. You feel it – as I have told you – in your heart. Inside down deep. You feel its indestructibility. After your body is dead, you'll feel it.'

'Then my body must die some day?' I asked.

'Only if you will it,' he said.

'And will I will it?'

'Yes,' he said. 'You'll want to, long before you actually do.'

'Why?'

'Because of what you'll know of things that lie beyond the world of human beings.'

Later on, I asked him if the others were going to do the same things as I, and he said: 'No.'

'Why have I been chosen out of the ten?' I asked.

'Because you were the only one who could hope to understand fully.'

'I don't understand you.'

'Listen to me,' he said. 'There is a town in Jehoraz not far from the old glory of Judea where an old Jew lived. He was very old and he knew that soon he would die, so he

141

had his grave dug before he died to make certain that it would be just as he wanted it. When the grave-digger had finished, the Jew went to the grave and looked down into it and he shook his head and said: This grave will not do at all. The grave-digger was surprised. He'd worked hard and he considered it a good job, well done. So he said: What is wrong with this grave? Then the old Jew replied: I cannot lie in a grave like this. It is much too narrow and much too deep. When the day of resurrection comes, how shall I be able to scale the sides of it and come forth? With the bottom so deep, I'll not be able to climb out. With the sides so narrow, I'll not be able to get a foothold. So the grave-digger made the grave shallower and widened the sides, and the old Jew was satisfied and returned home to die.'

Cambreau paused and took breath.

'It's much the same way with the men here,' he said. 'Except for you, each of them lies in a grave that is too narrow and too deep. They can't get up and come out of it. The grave is humanness. They're steeped in it, each of them, and they can climb up only a little way but they can't get all the way out of it.'

'And I can?' I asked.

'You have,' he said.

12

The evening of the fourteenth day, we reached Santiago de Cuba. There was an indefinable thrill seeing a destination come out of the smoky rise of distant land. And then, as darkness fell, the lights came up and twinkled and put the stars to shame.

We docked in a basin where there were a lot of other schooners, open boats and fishing smacks. Each had its own slip and after we furled our sails we used the engine to put our nose into a vacant slip ourselves. A dark-skinned man came up to the dock where our prow touched and grinned toothily and said: 'Hello there. Make fast and then you can come and register.' He spoke Spanish.

After we had made fast, I took Telez to the small box-house headquarters where the dark-skinned man sat down with a pen in his hand. 'Name of the ship?'

'*Albatross,*' I said.

'Rig?'

'Schooner.'

'Owner?' he asked.

'Well –' I began.

He glanced up and frowned. 'Yes?'

'Philip LaSalle,' I said.

'Philip LaSalle,' he said repeating. 'Home port?'

'Port of Spain, Trinidad,' I said.

'Very good,' he said. 'How long do you expect to be berthed here?'

'Perhaps a day or two,' I said.

'Very good,' he grinned again and nodded his head as

he spoke. 'The charge for the slip is twenty cents a day. That includes water.'

'That will be fine,' I said.

'Sign here, if you please.'

I took the pen and signed the registration card. Then he took it and filed it in his cabinet. *'Americano?'* he asked: 'Are you an American?'

'Yes,' I replied.

'Yusted?' he asked Telez.

'He's Spanish,' I said. *'Español.'*

'Ah,' said the registrar. 'Is that so? You are sailing for the sport no doubt?'

'Yes,' I said. 'For the sport.'

'Did you cross from Spain?'

'Oh well,' I said evasively, 'we've been sailing just about everywhere.'

'Listen,' Telez interrupted, 'perhaps you can help me, *señor*. I have a cousin in Santiago. Pedro Dominguez de las Salinas.'

'I don't know him,' said the registrar.

'He lives on Calle de Angeles,' Telez said. 'Can you tell me how I get there?'

The registrar could and did. When he had finished, Telez turned to me abruptly and said: 'Good-bye.' Then he started to walk off.

'Wait a minute,' I said. 'Don't walk off like that. When will you be back?'

'I'm not coming back,' he said.

'What?'

'I'm not coming back. I'm going to stay here. I may as well. When I get more money I'll go back home. Until I get it, I'll stay with my cousin. He'll take care of me.'

'You won't be back at all?'

'No,' Telez said. 'I've had enough.' He walked off without another word and disappeared, leaving me disappointed and flabbergasted.

I went back to the registrar who showed an annoying

inclination to be curious. I stopped him by arranging to have the water tanks and the gasoline tanks filled. When that was done, I went back to the boat.

Weiner and DuFond showed no real desire to leave, despite the fact that they had been on the sea for fourteen days. Later, however, they went off talking together in a comradely fashion which had been foreign to them before. They promised to return within a couple of hours to spend the night on board. Flaubert stayed in the cabin. Pennington sat up on deck with Cambreau. I joined them and asked: 'Where's Benet?'

'Oh,' Pennington said, 'he sneaked out right after we landed.'

'He did?' I felt nervous.

'Yes, while you and Telez were up with that fellow. What was all that anyway?'

'I had to register the boat,' I replied. 'It's in my name. Is that all right?'

'Of course. Where did Telez go?'

'He went to see his cousin. He isn't coming back. You shouldn't have let Benet leave.'

Pennington looked surprised. 'Telez – you mean he's through with the schooner?'

I nodded.

'He's finished his escape. He's here safe and sound.'

'That's rather abrupt,' Pennington said, somewhat sadly. 'I mean – he might have said good-bye or something – as long as he's not coming back.'

I shrugged. 'Well, he didn't.' Then I chuckled and glanced at Cambreau. 'Probably he avoided us because he still considers you a minion of the nether regions.'

Cambreau laughed.

'Just the same,' Pennington said, 'he might have said goodbye.'

A smile crept across Cambreau's lips. 'Jesus will come back,' he said. 'He'll come back to-night.'

'I hope so,' Pennington sighed. 'I'd like to say good-bye to him.'

'I wish Benet were here,' I said soberly.

We sat there without speaking for a while. Some one on one of the boats was strumming a guitar and singing throatily in Spanish. The slips had a smell of fish around them. It wasn't a particularly clean waterfront. Every now and then a block of light reflected from one of the other boats illuminated the water and we'd see patches of garbage, fruit skins or a dead fish or two float past.

'Is either of you going into town to-night?' I asked finally.

'Not I,' Pennington replied.

Cambreau shook his head.

I sighed and got up. 'I think I will,' I said. 'I feel like walking. I'll try to find Benet and bring him back. He shouldn't be out alone.'

'Go ahead,' Pennington said pleasantly. 'But don't get lost.'

'I'll be careful,' I said. 'Sure you don't want to come?'

'No thanks. I'll sit here and consider my penal survey.'

'By the way,' I inquired, 'are you going to write it? I hadn't heard you mention it for some time.'

Pennington smiled sadly. 'I'll never write it, I just like to think about it. It would make no difference if I wrote it. It would be real only to those who knew it and they are the only ones who would not be able to get hold of it. I think it would be very comprehensive, unimportantly so. However, the project is beyond me. I'd never finish it.'

I decided suddenly not to go into town and sat down again. 'Why do you say that?' I asked.

'Because it's the truth,' he said. 'I never finish things. I dream about them, but I never finish them. I've never finished anything I've ever started.'

'Well,' I said, 'you've finished your escape anyhow.'

He shrugged. 'But have I? . . . . What is escape to me? I can't get away from it myself.'

146

'Must you?' Cambreau asked.

Pennington didn't answer that, and I thought he looked embarrassed, so I said: 'Listen, Pennington, what are you going to do?'

'Do?'

'Yes. I mean – where are you going?'

'Last stop. America, I guess.'

'But then where?'

'I don't know,' he said.

'Have you a home?'

'You mean am I married? No . . .' He stopped and rubbed his chest reflectively. 'Frankly I had rather counted on dying, but that seems to have been changed by some one.' He glanced at Cambreau. 'It upset my plans.'

Cambreau was brazenly innocent. 'What a pity!' he exclaimed ingenuously.

'It was almost,' Pennington said, 'as if I'd been spared for a purpose.'

'What purpose?' I asked.

'I'm not sure,' Pennington replied. 'But you see, I hadn't counted on living, and therefore, I made no plans. It seems now that I must make a plan if I hope to survive at all.'

'There is suicide,' Cambreau said.

'That's ridiculous,' Pennington said. 'You don't destroy your life when it's been handed back to you.'

I said: 'Perhaps you're really meant to finish that penal survey after all.'

'I don't fancy it's that important,' Pennington remarked. He watched Cambreau. 'What's your guess?'

'Well,' Cambreau said, 'it would seem conceivable that you are being preserved so that you may lend yourself to others.'

'How?'

'Your understanding of metaphysics is astonishing for a man who has been schooled so soundly in human sciences. That is a project which you might finish. I think that would be important.'

Pennington reflected. It made quite an impression on him. He made no reply and after a time excused himself, plainly engrossed in profound thought, and went below for the night. No sooner had he vanished from the deck, than we heard the thud of running feet across the boards of the pier and presently we saw Jesus Telez emerge from the gloom, breathing raucously, his face pallid, his eyes brimming with dread. He jumped on to the deck and ran recklessly astern, skipping nimbly over the coaming to where we sat. He did not look at me at all but grabbed Cambreau by the arm and cried out in a frenzy: '*Venga usted! Venga usted!* You've got to come with me! Hurry and come!'

'Hello,' Cambreau said. 'Sit down and catch your breath, Jesus.'

'I cannot! I cannot!' Telez's eyes rolled agonizingly. 'She's dying.' His voice dropped, became taut and low. 'She is dying, *señor*. It is the fever.'

'What are you saying?' I asked.

'Conchita,' Telez said. 'My cousin's smallest. It is the fever. When I reached there to-night, she was lying there dying. Pedro told me she had been sick with the fever for three days. The doctor can do nothing. He says it is hopeless. He says she will die before to-morrow.'

Cambreau asked: 'Why did you come back here, Jesus?'

'I came for you!' Telez said. 'You can stop it! You can heal her! God of mercy, you can heal her. You are the only one.'

'But you have believed that I am a devil,' Cambreau said.

'Forgive me,' Telez said, pleading. He went down on his hands and kissed Cambreau's hands. 'God forgive me!'

'You said I was a devil.'

148

'I know, I know, but you aren't! I was wrong, you aren't a devil. You are an angel!'

'Sit down,' Cambreau said.

Telez hesitated.

'Sit down,' Cambreau said. 'And take that fear from your eyes.'

Telez sat down. He clenched his hands together and extended them. 'Please – please –'

'You're still afraid,' Cambreau said. 'If you know that I can heal her, why are you afraid?'

There was a moment of silence while Telez slowly straightened up and watched Cambreau. He fought with himself and finally said: 'I'm not afraid.'

'That's good,' Cambreau said. 'There's no reason to be afraid. Conchita isn't going to die.'

There was a faint scraping whisper . . . 'No?'

Cambreau shook his head. 'You love her?'

Telez nodded. 'I saw her to-night for the first time. She was so small. She is only four. Her face was red and her head was hot –'

'It's cool now,' Cambreau said. 'She's asleep. To-morrow morning she'll get up as though nothing had happened at all. She won't even remember it. Go back to your cousin, Jesus, and tell him that. . . . Let the child alone. Let her sleep. And to-morrow morning when she awakens and you see that there is no fever in her face, remember this. Remember that *I* did not do it. Remember that *you* did it because you loved her. That's why she'll be well, Jesus, because that love you have for her is God.'

Telez rose slowly to his feet saying: '*Gracias.* I'll remember. Good night. . . . Good night, Doctor.'

'Good night,' I said.

I watched Telez walk away until he reached the end of the pier and the shadows swallowed him.

13

Benet did not return all night long. Weiner, who was first to rise next morning, saw that the bunk had not been slept in at all. 'What do you suppose happened to Louis?' he asked.

No one replied. No one knew, but each of us could imagine and we were disturbed. All except Flaubert, who didn't care. I told them that I would take a look around the city and see if I could locate him. Weiner couldn't resist saying, with a grin: 'Don't miss the jails.'

Pennington cooked us a good breakfast and then we went up on the stern and sat around torpidly looking the waterfront over. It was the first time we had seen it by daylight. It hadn't changed much from the night before. The buildings and scenery looked grey, relieved only by the cloudless sky and warm brilliant sunlight. We talked a while and decided that we would weigh anchor and depart the next day. There was no sense just lying in a slip.

Pretty soon someone on the pier shouted a cheery: 'Hello, men!' and we all looked up quickly to see the familiar figure of Roy Meredith. I was pleasantly surprised because I had – frankly – forgotten about him and the fact that he had planned to meet us here. He came on board and was welcomed heartily. He shook hands with all of us and accepted a cup of Pennington's coffee. He was glad to see us and he had brought an American newspaper, the Miami *World-News*. He showed us his story, and we read it. It was well written, mentioned us all, and there was even a picture of the schooner which he had procured. Of course we weren't in it. And he had made no mention of the fact that we had intended sailing to Cuba from Port of Spain. Meredith was a regular guy. I liked him. He told us how he had flown to Santiago a week before and had been waiting for us with no little trepidation. He told us all the news.

Later he had a word alone with me. 'I put the total of the escape party at eleven,' he confided, 'and I want to tell you the NNA nearly had my hide for it. I told you that the official list of escaped was ten and they wanted to know where I got off adding an extra. I told them that there had been eleven in the boat, no matter how many were supposed to have escaped and the fact that I was getting my information first hand was the only thing that placated them. As a matter of fact, I had an answer to my cable the day after you sailed and I want to tell you, the French office in the Guiana said that no Jean Cambreau had escaped from the colony, no Jean Cambreau had ever been in the colony, and no Jean Cambreau had ever been heard of in their records. It makes no difference to me, of course, but I thought you might be interested to know. As I remember, you were a little puzzled about the man yourself.'

'I was,' I said, 'but not any more.'

'Oh,' he said, 'you know who he is then?'

'Not yet,' I said. 'But I'm beginning to know.'

'I see,' Meredith said. But he didn't. 'You know, he's a strange sort of guy. Sort of compelling. You know what I mean. When I saw him that first time in Port of Spain, he made me feel all – well – I can't describe it –'

'I know,' I said.

'I had an idea that he was motivated,' he said – 'that sounds silly, but that's it – motivated by something terrific. I had the same feeling this morning when I shook hands with him. He gets the feeling across to you somehow and you feel as though you've had a shot of hop or something. It just gives you a kind of lift. Know what I mean?'

'Yes,' I said.

'What kind of a trip did you have?' he asked. 'Anything exciting?'

'Nothing at all,' I said. 'Flaubert fell overboard once and DuFond pulled him out. That was the only thing. It so happened that the wind had died and we were standing still, but it took pluck just the same because there were sharks.'

'Sharks!' His eyes glowed. 'Good stuff!'

'Oddly,' I said, 'that was the first and last time I saw a shark at all during the entire voyage.'

'Say,' Meredith exclaimed, 'you ought to be a newspaper man yourself. This is good copy. Anything else?'

'No,' I said. 'Really nothing. I wish there were something more so that we might repay you for everything. But that's the story. There have been changes, of course, but you wouldn't write about those.'

'Changes?'

'Yes.'

'What kind of changes?' he asked. 'I don't get you.'

'Changes in the men,' I said. 'In each one of us. You couldn't write about those. You know how it is. Private worlds of our own. Each man has his. Most of them have been changed by – well, by the experience.'

'Oh,' he said. He grinned. 'Deep stuff . . . Well, this last stretch certainly has made the pack of you bloom. Honestly, I never saw such a healthy bunch of men. Well, where do you go from here?'

I smiled. 'That's one thing I can't tell you,' I said. 'You've got to be a good sport and let us finish at Santiago de Cuba. From now on, the escape is going to disintegrate. One by one we're reaching our destinations. It will be better if we do that anonymously, without any notoriety at all. You can say that we were last seen in the schooner heading north from the Windward Passage.'

'All right,' he agreed. 'When do you sail again?'

'To-morrow. We just decided.'

152

'Will you have dinner with me to-night?' he asked.

'All right,' I said.

'I'll come back here for you. Around five-thirty . . . I'd like to take the whole gang, but after all, I'm practically a pauper.'

'They'll understand,' I said. 'You've done enough.'

'I'll come back then. So long.' He waved good-bye again from the pier and then went into the city.

Telez came a little later. He looked like a different man. He was smiling from ear to ear and it lifted his cheeks up into his eyes. He went to Cambreau and he kissed his cheek.

'Hello,' Cambreau said.

Telez sat down beside him and watched him with adoration in his dark eyes. Then he asked softly: 'Tell me what I must do. . . . How can I be forgiven?'

'Forgiven?' Cambreau inquired. 'Why should you be forgiven?'

'For calling you a devil,' Telez said.

'Oh,' Cambreau laughed. 'That! That is nothing to be forgiven for. If I forgave you for that, I would imply that I was a better man than you are.'

'*Es verdad,*' Telez said.

'No,' said Cambreau. 'No man is better than another man. We are all the same, every one of us. Remember that. There is nothing which I have done that you cannot do also.'

'You are holy,' Telez said.

'Holier-than-thou?' Cambreau asked.

'No, I mean you are righteous.'

'All right, I'm righteous. But not self-righteous. I am righteous as every man is, you yourself, basically.'

'Then gratitude,' Telez said. 'How can I express to you my gratitude for this thing? I must do something.'

'You can believe,' Cambreau replied, 'what I told you last night. God is the love a man expresses to his fellow men. Believe that, and when you believe it, practise it.

153

. . . Let that be your gratitude and your life.'

'*Bueno,*' Telez said. 'I will try to do that.'

He said good-bye to us all, shook hands with each one of us, and then left.

I never saw him again.

14

There were empty hours that day, full of nothing to do. We did not need to stock the boat. We had enough food left in the galley. The water supply had been replenished. Nothing prevented our sailing away except our own decision, and when the afternoon grew unbearably hot, we were sorry we had to put it off until the next day. Meanwhile we worried a great deal about Louis Benet. He had not returned to the boat since he had left it the night before. We were aware that he might have decided to remain on the island, feeling that escape – as far as he was concerned – was finished. But somehow I felt that we would see him again. I think Cambreau gave me that impression.

Meredith called for me at the boat for dinner. It was uncomfortable and I regretted having to put on my white coat. The heat had made us all sticky. Meredith and I went into the city and dined at a fairly decent hotel. The food was good. Most of the time we talked and darkness fell while we were at it.

We were sipping our coffee and waiting for dessert when another man came over to our table and said hello to Meredith.

'Here's a yarn for you to cover,' the man said. Meredith told me later his name was Page and that he was a United Press correspondent. 'I just picked it up at headquarters. Some guy raped a ten-year-old girl and then committed suicide. He kept the kid in a lousy little dump since last night. She damn near died.'

'No kidding,' Meredith exclaimed, owl-eyed. He rose from his chair. 'When'd you get this?'

'Ten minutes ago,' Page told him, 'I was over at police headquarters when a Latin from Manhattan came in squawling about the corpse that was spoiling the scenery across the way from him. We all went back and found the guy there. He didn't have anything on to identify him. . . . You might run over. They're still there. I couldn't stay myself.'

'Where is it?'

'Buena Vista. Number four-ten. It's a pretty mangy neighbourhood. You'll see the crowd.'

I got up. 'I want to come with you.'

'Swell,' Meredith said. 'Let's go. Mind missing dessert?'

'No. Let's go.'

He paid the bill and I thanked him as he steered me through the city towards Calle de Buena Vista. Page had been right. When we arrived we saw the curious crowd standing around in front of a squalid little hovel. They were talking all at once and the result was a loud monotone. Lots of children were running around screaming shrilly to each other. The police held them back. Meredith pushed his way through the crowd with me in tow and confidently showed a press card to the police. We passed through the lines and entered the house. The hall was dark and dirty. We climbed groaning stairs to the second floor where we met more police. We walked by them and into the room. Like the rest of the place it was buried in grey dirt. It didn't look as though it had ever been cleaned. It had a washstand and a white enamel basin, only the basin wasn't white any more. It was streaked with brown dirt and had a water-line that could never have been washed off. There was a bed in one corner covered with a pair of rumpled sheets. A policeman – he appeared to be in charge – was standing beside it looking down at a black-haired girl who was lying all curled up in a daze and crying. Her face looked older than the policeman's beside her. Page had said she was ten years old. Her body was immature, her chest flat, her hips very small. I found a doctor conversing quietly with one of the policemen. 'We'll have to get her to a hospital. . . .' The policeman said: 'We've got to find out what happened first.' 'Over here,' Meredith said, pulling me. 'The guy is in this closet over there.'

I followed him over to the single closet before which two policemen were standing. They moved aside for us and said something in Spanish. Meredith looked in and whistled. 'Gosh!' I looked in too. Benet was hanging from a hook in the closet. Round his throat were a pair of shoe laces interlaced for strength. His eyes were wide open and popping gruesomely. His arms and legs hung straight down. His shoes were off, on the floor, without laces. His whole face was horribly contorted. Somehow, though, I couldn't feel shocked.

'He met me on the street,' the child said later when she had stopped crying, 'and he promised to give me something if I came with him. So I went and he brought me up here and I got scared and cried and he said: If you don't stop crying I'll kill you. Then I stopped crying because I was afraid and then . . . he did it. I told him I wanted my mother and he said: All right, I'll get her for you and he said: What's your name? Then I told him my name was Marion Benet. *What did he do after that?* He didn't say anything at all, he just stared at me a long time and then he went to the closet and hit his head and cried out something. I didn't know what, and then he took off his shoes and tied the laces together. I was afraid he was going to do something to me again but he went in the closet and then I heard a lot of funny noises like he was choking and I got so scared I couldn't keep quiet any more and I cried and cried and then a different man came in and saw everything and ran out again.'

'The guy who told the cops,' Meredith said. 'Poor kid.'

There were voices all over the room. The doctor: 'That's all. Get her to the hospital.' The policeman: 'Easy with her there. Carry her easy.' Another policeman:

'How about the man?' The head policeman: 'Cut him down now. Anybody know who he is?'

Nobody knew. Meredith didn't remember seeing him in Port of Spain. Benet had been in jail when Meredith visited us on the pier there.

'Anyway,' Meredith said vindictively, 'he strangled to death. Those shoestrings didn't break his filthy neck. I hope he had a long time dying. Too bad we can't get his name. A news story is like a flat tyre when there're no names. . . . Let's go.'

We left.

When I returned to the schooner later than night, I told the men that I had seen Benet and that he was not sailing with us. I gave them the impression that he was quite satisfied with Santiago de Cuba and they asked no questions. But up in the stern, later, I sat alone with Cambreau while the others slept and I said to him: 'Did you know this would happen?'

'Yes,' he said. 'I did.'

'But what of the child?' I asked. 'How can –'

He shrugged. 'She won't remember.'

'But the agony –'

'All gone,' he said. 'The doctors will be amazed.'

'It was a terrible thing,' I said.

'A similarity of names,' Cambreau said, 'made him understand himself.'

'Oh,' I said thoughtfully. 'Then she – it wasn't his own daughter?'

'Nothing so fateful,' Cambreau said.

So Benet's change came, with grim finality. In those last moments, thinking the child his daughter, he had seen all his other crimes in a blinding flash of repentance. His death bore mute testimony to his change.

15

We sailed the next morning at ten o'clock. It was a very quiet departure. Meredith came to the dock and said good-bye to us and wished us luck. I thanked him for the dinner and everything else and told him I hoped that some day we'd see each other again. Then we started the auxiliary engine and backed slowly out of the slip. We went down the bay and within an hour we had reached the open sea and headed east towards the Windward Passage and Cape Maysi. As soon as we had cleared the harbour, we stopped the engine and broke out the sails. A good wind picked us up and carried us along. It stayed with us, too, the rest of the way.

The second day out, something happened to Cambreau and it worried me. That morning, I found him crying in his bunk. His shoulders shook and tears stained his pillow. It was an awkward situation. I never liked to see a man cry. Even Flaubert went out of his way to notice it. He sat up in his bunk and stopped his monotonous repetition of the tribulations of poor Rudolph and blinked in amazement at Cambreau's back.

I touched Cambreau and asked: 'What's wrong?'

He twisted away and cringed back in the corner of his bunk exclaiming sharply: 'Leave me alone! Leave me alone!'

'What's the matter with you?' I asked.

'None of your business!' he said, waving me back. 'Go away and leave me alone. You only want to hurt me! You all want to hurt me! You've hated me all the time and now you want to hurt me!'

'Stop it!' I said tersely. 'You're making a fool of yourself!'

'You only want to hurt me! Leave me alone!'

DuFond came over. 'We don't want to hurt you, Cambreau.'

'Yes you do! You all do! You want to hurt me!'

Weiner looked sad. He shook his head and went up on deck. Pennington frowned.

'You all hated me from the beginning.'

Flaubert stared at him.

Later Pennington said to me: 'I think he's shamming.'

I said: 'If he is, he's doing an admirable job. But why on earth should he emulate a man with a nervous breakdown? Why, he's as bad as Flaubert!'

'That's it,' Pennington said. 'I believe that's why he's doing it.'

'What do you mean?'

'Well,' he said, 'didn't you see how Flaubert sat up and took notice when Cambreau cried?'

'Yes,' I said. 'He did sit up.'

'And if you've noticed, he hasn't opened his mouth all day about himself. He even ate with us. That's the first time since we left the colony that he's eaten through an entire meal with us and not bolted or imagined some persecution.'

Cambreau kept it up. He refused his meals that day and he stayed below. Each time I went down, his shoulders were shaking and Flaubert was watching him with concern.

The thing went on a third day and then a fourth. By this time, after skirting the northern coast of Cuba, we had reached Cocos Key where we left the island behind us and steered a north-west course across the Great Bahama Bank for America.

I was sitting at the helm with Weiner that afternoon when Flaubert poked his head timidly out of the cabin and looked at us. I smiled at him and said: 'Hello.'

'Hello,' he answered warily.

'Hello,' Weiner said pleasantly. 'Come on up here. The sun feels good.'

Flaubert debated for a while and then came up. He didn't sit too close to us. He looked around the horizon and breathed deeply a few times.

Finally I asked: 'How is Cambreau?'

Flaubert shook his head sadly.

'Is he still crying?' I asked.

He nodded.

Nothing more was said for some time until he suddenly blurted out: 'Doctor, can't you do something for him?'

Weiner looked at me, trying to conceal his surprise.

'What can *I* do?' I asked Flaubert.

'Someone ought to do something,' he said. 'He makes me shiver. He's been crying all the time.'

'There's nothing we can do,' I said. 'That's what happens when a man thinks about himself too much instead of thinking about others.'

'But he keeps crying,' Flaubert said. 'He keeps saying that we all want to hurt him and that we all hate him. . . . I don't want to hurt him. Do you?'

'No,' I said.

'Of course not,' Weiner added.

'You don't hate him either, do you?'

'No,' I repeated.

'I don't hate him,' Flaubert said. 'I always thought he was a nice man. He was very nice to me when we were in Trinidad. He took me with him one night and we went for a long walk. On the way, he met a crippled boy and he healed him. . . . It makes me feel badly to see him cry like that. You see, he's crying about nothing at all.'

'That's it,' I said. 'He's afraid of something that doesn't exist. We don't hate him. We wouldn't hurt him. But apparently he's been thinking about himself and he has lost his sense of perspective. If he could forget himself and think of his friends and lend himself to them instead of keeping himself to himself, this wouldn't happen. He's made a graven image. He's made a god of himself. He's holding his pity and humility and love all for himself and

161

that's why an illusion, something that doesn't exist at all, has terrified him so and made him so unhappy.'

Flaubert sighed. 'I wish we could do something.'

'You know,' I said guardedly, 'that was what troubled you once before you *changed*.' I could see Weiner hold his breath and watch Flaubert.

Flaubert nodded after an interminable wait. 'Yes,' he said. 'I can see that now. . . . How silly it seems when you look back on it.'

'Yet,' I said, 'it's as real to Cambreau at this moment as it was to you.'

'I wish you could help him,' Flaubert said anxiously.

'I can't,' I said, 'but you could. . . .'

'I?' He sounded puzzled, but eager.

'Yes,' I said. 'You've been through it. You know how futile, how selfish, how empty it is. If you told him what you had learned, he might believe you.'

'Do you think he would?'

'I do,' I said. 'What do you think, Weiner?'

Weiner nodded. 'I think it would turn the trick.'

'I don't know,' Flaubert murmured doubtfully.

'It's an awful thing,' I said. 'You know how it affected you. You might save him that.'

Flaubert sat for several minutes considering it. He didn't say a word. At length, he got up, smiled at us reassuringly, and went down into the cabin.

He stayed down there until nightfall. When he came up once more, Cambreau was with him. They were both smiling broadly and their arms were linked. I looked at Cambreau whose eyes returned my stare with sparkling slyness. 'Flaubert,' he said with his natural cheerfulness, 'has shown me the error of my ways. I shall be indebted to him forever.'

'No indebtedness,' Flaubert said. 'I'm only glad I could do something to show you how false your thought was.'

'You certainly did that,' Cambreau said. 'You healed me.'

It made Flaubert very happy.

16

We were nearing the end now. Eight days from Santiago de Cuba and in the twilight, we slipped slowly past the government channel out into the port of Miami and swung out around the peninsula and kept north, the wind continuing moderate. Just before darkness, we could see long miles of clean sandy beach stretching up the coast, and in the distance, silhouetted by the dropping sun, the skyscrapers of the city stood out against the sky. The same wind that filled our sails gently swayed the lines of palm trees which stood like fence posts all along the streets behind the beach. No one took any notice of us. We were like any one of the smaller craft which, at the moment, were tied up in the City Basin and down at the docks of the Royal Palm Club. The lights of the city came up as we continued. They were gay lights; some of them were multi-coloured, some – covering an old sailing ship – patterned the outline of the wind-jammer with numerous bulbs.

We had plotted, meanwhile, how the escape – now at an end – should disintegrate. It was safer if each man went off alone, never to see the rest again. Thus in the new life before us, we would not remind each other of the past, or threaten each other with it. We decided to go over the side – one by one – along the shore at far points, swimming to land alone so that our respective arrivals would excite no curiosity or suspicion.

When the darkness was complete we lowered the sails, furled them, and started the auxiliary engine. Cambreau handled the ship, sitting at the helm. It was a solemn occasion. DuFond was the first to go. He said good-bye to each one of us, shook hands, and wished us all good luck. Cambreau steered in towards shore as far as it was safe to go. Then he cut the speed, and DuFond, waving a last good-bye from the bow, steadied himself and dived far out and away from us with hardly any splash at all. We saw his head come up and watched his arms stroke the water rhythmically as he swam into shore and disappeared from sight.

Cambreau throttled the engine again and we moved up the shore a long way until he cut it again and let us drift. Weiner made his good-byes. He was weeping. He felt the occasion deeply and wasted no time prolonging it. As soon as he had finished, he stepped over the railing into the sea and swam away hastily and somewhat amateurishly, his shoulders jerking from side to side.

Farther up the shore, Flaubert went off, beaming happily. He was very anxious to get ashore. He shook hands with us, said 'Good-bye! Good-bye all! God bless you all!' and dived in. He swam dextrously. It surprised me a little.

Pennington did not want to go. It saddened him. He sat with us a long time after Cambreau cut the engine and let the boat drift, the mute signal for the plunge. There wasn't anything to say. Sentences were strained and didn't mean anything. He realized it finally and got up, sighing. He didn't shake hands at all. He just looked at us both and said: 'I'm sure we'll meet again somewhere, Doctor. And Cambreau – that project – I promise you that I'll finish it.' He nodded casually to us and slowly lowered himself into the water. As he started to swim away easily on his side, he called back: 'It takes your breath away at first. It's a trifle cool.' And then he was gone.

We started once again.

'You remember,' Cambreau said, 'what I told you you would do?'

'Yes,' I said.

'Your life,' he said. 'That's what I mean. You remember all that.'

'Yes, I remember,' I replied.

'And the book, you read it.'

'I practised it,' I said.

'I know. You had more to do with Flaubert's recovery than I did. I knew you would help him. . . . You believe you are ready?'

'I know I am,' I said.

'Well, that's all then.'

There was a short pause. He throttled down the engine. I went down into the cabin and came up with Moll's Bible in my hands. 'I won't take this,' I said. 'The sea would ruin it. I'll leave it with you. I can't forget the words anyhow.'

'I'll keep it,' he said and took it from me. We were drifting slowly now. I could see the line of the shore where the small waves reached the sand.

I asked: 'Where will you go now?'

'To look for a worthy house,' he said.

'And I shall never see you again?' I said.

'You know better, he said. 'You know there is no time, no space, in love. Remember me and when you give yourself to others, you will see me every time.'

'I know,' I said. I walked to the railing and stepped over the side and slowly lowered myself. The water was cold. It rose up my legs to my hips and there it stopped as I clung for a moment and called: 'Jean!'

'Yes,' he asked.

'I wanted you to know,' I said, 'that I have recognized who you are at last.'

He smiled the ageless smile. 'People will recognize you for the same,' he said. 'Good-bye!'

'Good-bye,' I said, and I dropped into the sea.

17

When I had reached a depth inshore where my feet could touch bottom, I stopped swimming and started to walk slowly from the surf. The sea felt clean and fresh and I was sorry to feel it recede from me as I slowly waded out on to the hard damp sand at the water's edge. There I stood for a moment and turned to glance out at the schooner.

It was moving directly eastward towards the Bahamas, clearly outlined against the white moon. Cambreau was standing in the stern by the helm, a slight black figure, behind the cabin. The schooner looked small then, like a tick crawling across the belly of the ocean.

Then I heard the dry sand away from the water crunch loudly and I turned and saw a man running down the beach. He was running hard and every now and then, the sucking sand would make him stumble. Once he fell, face down and grunted when he hit. But it didn't dismay him. He picked himself up and ran hard again. In the moonlight, his face was pale.

When he saw me he swerved swiftly in my direction and when he finally reached me, he grabbed my arm in frantic hopefulness and exclaimed hoarsely: 'My son – he's been hurt – a car struck him –' He tried to catch his breath. 'I think he's dying – Are you a doctor?'

I looked into his eyes.

'No,' I said.

'I must get a doctor!' he said.

He flung my arm back and started to run down the beach again. After he had gone about twenty yards he slowed down, halted, paused wonderingly, and then came back, walking with long measured steps. He stopped in front of me, looked down at my face, and asked huskily: 'Why did you look like that at me? . . . Who are you?'

'My name is Philip LaSalle,' I said, 'and I have come to heal your son.'